Insights from the Heart of a Shepherd

Acts

by
Ed White

ISBNs
eBook: 978-1-969506-70-3
Paperback: 978-1-969506-69-7
Hardcover: 978-1-969506-79-6

LCCN: 2025925277

Published by Kinetic Digital Publishers

www.kineticdigitalpublishers.com

For permissions, inquiries, or other correspondence, please visit our website.

TABLE OF CONTENTS

Introduction

"And He opened their understanding, that they might comprehend the Scriptures. Then He said to them, 'Thus it is written, and thus it was necessary for the Christ to suffer and to rise from the dead the third day, and that repentance and remission of sins should be preached in His name to all nations, beginning at Jerusalem. And you are witnesses of these things. Behold, I send the Promise of My Father upon you; but tarry in the city of Jerusalem until you are endued with power from on high.'" (Luke 24:45-49)

The book of Acts is about the church. It tells the story of how the Holy Spirit came upon the Apostles and directed them to establish the church in accordance with God's plan. He continued to direct them as the church developed and grew throughout the first generation of its existence on earth. If we want to understand the church as God designed it and as the Lord Jesus built it through His agents, the Apostles, we need to study the book of Acts. You should have your Bible at hand while you study so you can check the references. I use the NKJV, but any translation will do.

We begin with the 16th chapter of the gospel of Matthew, verses 16-19. "Simon Peter answered and said, 'You are the Christ, the Son of the living God.' Jesus answered and said to him, 'Blessed are you Simon Bar-Jonah, for flesh and blood has not revealed this to you, but my Father who is in heaven. And I also say to you that you are Peter, and on this rock, I will build My church, and the gates of Hades shall not prevail against it. And I will give you the keys of the kingdom of heaven, and whatever you bind on earth will be bound in heaven, and whatever you lose on earth will be loosed in heaven.'"

Now, I want you to mark the word rock in verse 18, Jesus said, "Upon this rock I will build My church." The rock of which He spoke was the fact that was stated by Simon Peter when he said, "You are the Christ, the Son of the Living God." That is the foundation upon which the church is built. The Bible tells us, "For no other foundation can anyone lay than that which is laid, which is Jesus Christ" (1 Corinthians 3:11). Those who teach that Peter was the rock upon which Christ built His church base that idea on the fact that the Greek word, Petros (translated Peter) means a small rock. On the other hand, the word translated rock (petra) in the phrase "upon this rock," means an underlying bedrock.

The bedrock upon which the church is founded, on which it rests, is that body of truth which we have in the Bible that tells us about Jesus Christ. This is where we begin our study of the church Jesus designed. Our understanding of that bedrock begins with the statement that He was in the beginning with the Father. He is eternal. He came into this world as Jesus of Nazareth. He was born in Bethlehem to a mother who was a virgin. He grew up in Nazareth and spent most of His life there. He conducted a ministry among the Israelites that lasted for a little over three years. During that time, He healed the sick, raised the dead, and taught many things about how we should live to be pleasing to God. The heart of the gospel is this: He died on a cross, was buried, and rose again on the third day. For forty days He appeared to many people showing He was alive again. Then He ascended into heaven where He is seated at the right hand of the Father, making intercession for us. This is a brief review of the body of facts, the truth on which the church was founded. Jesus is the Christ, the Son of the living God. He is the cornerstone upon which the church is built. Without Him there would be no church.

The second thing I want to point out to you is that Jesus said (and this was a promise He made to His apostles), "Upon this rock I will build My church." He promised to build His church; and He did build it. Right after that He said to the Apostles, "I will give you the keys of the kingdom of heaven and whatever you bind on earth will be what has already been bound in heaven" (Matthew 16:19). This is the Amplified Version, which has the most accurate translation of that sentence.

We understand that keys are used to open doors, and that the Apostles opened the doors to the kingdom by showing people how they could enter it. The juxtaposition of these two phrases, "the church" and "the kingdom of heaven," indicates to us that they are the same thing. Jesus Christ is the king, and those who have heard the gospel, have been obedient to it, and have committed their lives to walking day by day in the footsteps of Jesus, are the citizens of that kingdom; and they are the members of the church. The church and the kingdom are the same thing.

If you want further proof of that, let me point out to you the Parable of the Sower. In that parable, Jesus said the kingdom of heaven is like a Sower who went out to sow. He explained that the seed that was sown was the word of God. He describes four different conditions of the soil that received the seed; and those conditions of the soil correspond to the conditions of people's hearts when they receive the seed, the Word of God. The seed falls on good ground when hearts are fully prepared to receive it. They are transformed and produce the fruit of the Spirit. The seed that falls on ground that is not fully prepared ends up either choked out by the cares of this world or withered by the heat of persecution. They produce no fruit for the Lord. It is a perfect description of what happens when the church proclaims the truth and people receive it in one way or another.

The church and the kingdom are the same thing. One day the kingdom of heaven on earth will be taken up to heaven. When the Lord comes to receive His bride, the church, the kingdom of heaven on earth will become the kingdom of heaven at rest. As we sing in the song, "The church's one foundation is Jesus Christ her Lord." In another verse, it talks about the time when the church on earth will be the church at rest. That time is when we get to heaven. So, remember that the church and the kingdom of heaven are the same thing.

Turn to the gospel of John, chapter 14, verse 26. Jesus said these words to the disciples while they were still in the upper room where they had observed the Passover together; and Jesus had instituted the Lord's Supper. Judas had already left to go and meet with those enemies of Jesus to whom he would betray the Lord. Jesus said this to the eleven disciples who remained, "The Helper, the Holy Spirit whom the Father will send in My name, He will teach you all things and bring to your remembrance all things that I said to you." Jesus promised to send them the Holy Spirit who would guide them and enable them to remember everything He taught them. He would guide them into all truth.

Then, just before He ascended into heaven, Jesus said:

"Thus, it is written and thus it was necessary for the Christ to suffer and to rise from the dead the third day, and that repentance and remission of sins should be preached in His name to all nations, beginning at Jerusalem. And you are witnesses of these things. Behold, I send the promise of My Father upon you; but tarry in the city of Jerusalem until you are endued with power from on high." Luke 24:46-49

Before repentance and remission of sins could be preached in the name of Jesus; He had to die for us. Before He died for us, the message was "repent for the kingdom of heaven is at hand." In other words, "Repent and get ready because the kingdom is about to be established." But after He died and rose again, the message became "Repent and be baptized in the name of Jesus Christ for the remission of sins." Before that, they couldn't preach that message because He had not yet died for us.

He said to the apostles, "You are witnesses of these things." This occurred just before Jesus ascended into heaven. He had given them the commission. It is what we call the Great Commission, "Go therefore and make disciples of all the nations, baptizing them in the name of the Father and of the Son and of the Holy Spirit, teaching them to observe all things that I have commanded you and lo, I am with you always, even to the end of the age" (Matt. 28:19, 20). It is stated in the gospel of Mark, "Go into all the world and preach the gospel to every creature. He who believes and is baptized will be saved." He had given them the commission to take the gospel into all the world. But He said to them now, "Tarry in Jerusalem until you receive power from upon high. Then you will be My witnesses beginning in Jerusalem and going into all the world."

Chapter 1

The Church Jesus Built

"The former account I made, O Theophilus, of all that Jesus began both to do and teach until the day in which He was taken up after He through the Holy spirit had given the commandments to the Apostles whom He had chosen, to whom He also presented Himself alive after His suffering by many infallible proofs, being seen by them during forty days and speaking of things concerning the kingdom of God and being assembled with them, He commanded them not to depart from Jerusalem." Luke is restating what Jesus said in Luke 24. *"But wait for the promise of the Father which"* He said, *"You have heard from me, for John truly baptized with water but you shall be baptized with the Holy Spirit not many days from now"* **(Acts 1:1-5).**

Luke begins in Acts exactly where the gospel of Luke ended. He restates the story of the encounter of Jesus with His Apostles just before He ascended into heaven.

The promise of the Father, the baptism of the Holy Spirit, was promised to the Apostles. It wasn't promised to anybody else. "Therefore, when they had come together, they asked Him saying, 'Lord will you at this time restore the kingdom to Israel?'" (v. 6). They were thinking about the kingdom, but they were thinking about it in a different sense. They thought He was going to sit on a throne in the city of Jerusalem. He would be crowned the king; and the kingdom of the Messiah would be ushered into the world. They did not know His kingdom would be an eternal kingdom that would fill all the earth; and He wouldn't sit on a throne on earth, but He would be seated at the right hand of the Father in heaven. So, they asked, "Are you going to restore the kingdom at this time?" He responded, "It is not for you to know the times or the seasons which the Father has put in His own authority. But you shall receive power when the Holy Spirit has come upon you; and you shall be witnesses to Me in Jerusalem, and in all Judea and Samaria, and to the end of the earth" (vv. 7,8). In Luke He had said they would preach repentance and remission of sins in the name of Jesus, and that it would be to all the world; and here He says, "You'll be witnesses to me in Jerusalem, in Judea, in Samaria, and to the end of the earth." And while they watched, He was caught up and received into heaven, received out of their sight. They were standing there watching as He went up; and they continued to stand there looking up into the heavens. Two men, that is, two angels, then stood by them and said, "Why do you stand gazing up into heaven? This same Jesus, who was taken up from you into heaven, will so come in like manner as you saw Him go into heaven" (v. 11).

Ten days later they received the Holy Spirit. What did they do during those ten days? Mostly, they prayed. At that time, there were 120 followers of Jesus in Jerusalem. Luke names the eleven apostles, along with Mary, the mother of Jesus, and others who met together in an upper room. I don't think anyone had a room big enough to hold 120 people. It's most likely that when the 120 gathered together, they were in the temple. That would be the easiest place for them to go and gather with a group that size.

During that time there was one other thing they did. They selected a successor for Judas. Luke tells us how they did that beginning in verse 15. He says that Peter stood up in the midst of the disciples, the 120, and said to them, "Men and brethren, the Scripture had to be fulfilled, which the Holy Spirit spoke before by the mouth of David concerning Judas who became a guide to those who arrested Jesus." Peter pointed out that the scriptures teach that there would be one selected to take his place. Then he gave the qualifications of those who could be successors to the Apostles. Beginning in verse 21 he says this, "Therefore, of these men who have accompanied us all the time that the Lord Jesus went in and out among us, beginning from the baptism of John to that day when He was taken up from us, one of these must become a witness with us of His resurrection." There were two qualifications. He had to be one who had traveled with them throughout the ministry of Christ, beginning with the baptism of John, until He was taken up from them into heaven; and he had to be an eyewitness of the resurrection. Apparently, there were only two people who fulfilled those qualifications. Those two were: a man named Joseph, who was also called Barsabas or Justus; and the second one was Matthias. They prayed and asked God to show them the one He had chosen. They then cast lots; and the lot fell on Matthias. From that day forward Matthias was counted as one of the twelve. (verses 24-26).

In this passage of scripture Peter makes it evident that anyone who became a successor to an Apostle had to fill these two qualifications. He had to have walked with them and traveled with them during the ministry of Jesus; and he had to have been an eyewitness to the resurrection. Obviously, nobody after that generation ever fulfilled those qualifications. There has never been anyone qualified to be a successor to the Apostles other than the one who was chosen that day and the second one who was not chosen. That's important, and we will see why later.

I want to close this chapter by pointing out how the first chapter of Acts closes and how the next chapter begins. When this was written it did not have chapter and verse designations. Those were inserted hundreds of years later. The chapter divisions were devised by Stephen Langton, Archbishop of Canterbury, in 1227 A.D. The verse divisions were not inserted until Robert Estienne did it in 1555 A.D. If you were reading this without these chapter and verse markings, you would see that the first verse of chapter two is a continuation of what was happening in the last verse of chapter one. In the last verse of chapter one, it says they cast their lots, and the lot fell on Matthias, and he was numbered with the eleven Apostles. In other words, he became the twelfth Apostle. Then it says that when the day of Pentecost had fully come, they were all with one accord in one place. To whom is it referring when it says they were all in one accord in one place? The nearest antecedent is the Apostles. That is who it is talking about, the Apostles. The next verse talks about how the Holy Spirit came upon them. Baptism of the Holy Spirit was promised to the Apostles and given to the Apostles and to no one else at that time. They were the chosen agents that Jesus used to build His church. He said, "Upon this rock I will build my church." Then He commissioned the twelve to be His agents in establishing the church according to His plan as they were directed by the Holy Spirit. I believe we should be diligent in our efforts to build the church in the twenty-first century to conform to the pattern given to us by the apostles. I want to be a part of a church that is trying to be like the church that is revealed to us in the scriptures.

Discussion Questions
Chapter 1

1. Why do you think the baptism of the Holy Spirit was only given to the apostles?

2. The apostles were given the power to heal people during the earthly ministry of Jesus. What do you think was different about the power they were given with the baptism of the Holy Spirit?

3. Was it God who directed the apostles to select a successor to Judas?

4. Why do you think it was important to have 12 apostles?

Chapter 2

The Church Is Born

"Therefore, let all the house of Israel know assuredly that God has made this Jesus, whom you crucified, both Lord and Christ.' Now when they heard this, they were cut to the heart, and said to Peter and the rest of the apostles, 'Men and brethren, what shall we do?' Then Peter said to them, 'Repent, and let every one of you be baptized in the name of Jesus Christ for the remission of sins; and you shall receive the gift of the Holy Spirit. For the promise is to you and to your children, and to all who are afar off, as many as the Lord our God will call.' And with many other words he testified and exhorted them, saying, 'Be saved from this perverse generation.' Then those who gladly received his word were baptized; and that day about three thousand souls were added to them. And they continued steadfastly in the apostles' doctrine and fellowship, in the breaking of bread, and in prayers." Acts 2:36-42

The occurrence described here happened in about 30 AD. (I refuse to use the modern designations, CE and BCE, which stand for Common Era and Before Common Era because they do not honor the name of Jesus Christ. BC and AD do honor His name. BC stands for Before Christ. AD is from Latin Anno Domini, meaning the Year of our Lord.) It is generally accepted that Jesus was actually born about 4 BC, so the date on which the church was born is calculated to 30 AD.

Concerning the term Pentecost, it was the widely used name of the Feast of Harvest, which was celebrated seven weeks after the Passover. The counting began on the day after the Sabbath.

The second chapter of the book of Acts divides naturally into three sections. The first section tells about the outpouring of the Holy Spirit upon the Apostles. It was the promise given to them by the Father. The second section is the sermon that Peter preached on that day of Pentecost. The third section describes the reaction of the people to Peter's sermon, including their decision to become followers of Jesus Christ. Three thousand of them were baptized into Christ that day.

In section one, three supernatural phenomena occurred along with the coming of the Holy Spirit. The first was the sound of a rushing, mighty wind that filled the house where they were sitting. I believe it is probably the thing that caused them to get up, and make their way to the temple. We do know that a little while later, they were in the temple. I think that when they heard that sound of the rushing mighty wind, they were convinced that the promise of the Father, which Jesus had told them to wait for, was coming. So, it was time to go to the temple and worship Him; and perhaps share the gospel message they were given with other people. How would you have reacted to the sound of a mighty rushing wind. The first thing I think about when I read those words is a hurricane or a tornado. In our part of the country, it would probably be a tornado. People almost always say tornadoes sound like a freight train. I take that to mean it's a rumbling roar of a sound, and accompanying that, there would be the sound of trees being uprooted and crashing to the ground, of debris being cast against the sides of buildings and against vehicles, and perhaps a few screams of terrified people. It would be an awful, frightening sound. I know that if I were outside and I heard a sound like that, the first thing I would do would be to look around. I would want to know the source of that sound. If that tornado is coming toward me or going away, I need to know. I would want to know if I needed to take shelter or if I'm going to be okay. What if you heard a sound like that, but you couldn't find any source for it? What if there wasn't even a stirring of a breeze, and the skies were bright blue? It would be very frightening. You would wonder where in the world that sound came from. I think the Apostles made their way to the temple when they heard that sound; and on the way they probably called out the rest of the 120 who were followers of Jesus in Jerusalem at that time. So altogether they made their way to the temple.

The second supernatural phenomenon was a fire that sat on the head of each of the twelve Apostles. How would you react if you had a flame of fire on your head? I have an idea that you'd be trying to slap it out. These men were no doubt bearded. If your hair caught on fire, and your beard caught on fire, chances are you wouldn't survive. So, you would want to put out that flame. But it would soon become apparent that even though there was a flame of fire sitting on each of their heads, none of them was being harmed. It wasn't burning their hair. It wasn't burning anything. It was just a flame on top of their heads. I believe the Israelites who saw that thought about the story of God speaking to Moses out of a bush that was on fire but not being consumed. It was part of their heritage. They would naturally have thought of that when they saw a fire that wasn't burning anything; and they may well have been intrigued by it. They knew that God spoke to Moses out of that burning bush. I wonder if they thought God was going to speak to them from these men with the flame on their heads that was not harming them.

About that time the apostles began to speak; and they spoke in all the languages of the people who were there that day. The second chapter of Acts lists sixteen different locations from which people had come to Jerusalem for the feast of ingathering, Pentecost. There were people from all over the Roman Empire, thousands of them in the temple. The Court of the Gentiles and the other courts inside the temple walls could hold as many as 100,000 people. One of those courts was the Court of Women. Although females were not allowed in the innermost court, they were permitted to enter that court. Luke does not tell us if women were included among the 3,000 who responded to the message of Peter. The apostles began to speak in all of the different languages. It's very interesting to see the word translated into the language in our versions. In the Greek original, it means dialects. They spoke in local dialects. That means that if you were from southern Egypt, they spoke to you in southern Egyptian, and if you were from Northern Phoenicia, they spoke to you in northern Phoenician.

People heard them speaking their own dialects. But there were skeptics. They were probably people who only spoke Aramaic; and they didn't realize that these were other languages; so, they said they were just babbling or drunk; and Peter used that idea to launch into his sermon. He said to them, "These men are not drunk as you suppose. After all, it's only 9:00 in the morning. But this is what is prophesied by Joel." He tells about God saying, "I will pour out My Spirit on all flesh." It's found beginning in Acts 2:17.

"And it shall come to pass in the last days, says God,
That I will pour out of My Spirit on all flesh;
Your sons and your daughters shall prophesy,
Your young men shall see visions,
Your old men shall dream dreams.
And on My menservants and on My maidservants
I will pour out My Spirit in those days;
And they shall prophesy.
I will show wonders in heaven above

And signs in the earth beneath:
Blood and fire and vapor of smoke.
The sun shall be turned into darkness,
And the moon into blood,
Before the coming of the great and awesome day of the Lord.
And it shall come to pass
That whoever calls on the name of the Lord
Shall be saved. "
Acts 2:17-21

This prophecy is like many prophecies. There is an immediate fulfillment and a delayed fulfillment. The immediate fulfillment was happening that day. This is the beginning, the pouring out of the Spirit upon men. From this point onward, they are directed by the Holy Spirit. They will dream dreams, see visions, and prophesy during the first generation of the church. When we come to chapter eight, we will see how that portion of the prophecy comes to an end.

The part about the sun turning into darkness and the moon into blood before the great and awesome day of the Lord refers to what's going to happen at the end of time. So, this prophecy began to be fulfilled that day and will continue until the end of time.

He says at the end of the prophecy, "Whoever calls on the name of the Lord shall be saved." That began that day. That was the day the gospel message was preached for the first time; and men came to understand that they could be saved from their sins because of Jesus Christ. A little while later, he tells them how to call on the name of the Lord. Beginning that day people could call on the name of the Lord and be saved. Now having told them what was happening, that this was a fulfillment of prophecy, he went on to tell them about Jesus. He pointed out that Jesus was well known among them. There were, no doubt, many in that crowd who had been healed by Jesus, perhaps hundreds of them. I feel sure Lazarus was there. He had been raised from the dead by Jesus just a few weeks earlier. These people knew about Jesus. They knew about His power. They knew what He had done. That's what Peter was saying to them. He was saying, "You know about Him. You know that His power testified that God approved of what He was doing." One of the Sanhedrin council members, Nicodemus had come to Jesus one night and said, "We know that no man can do the things you do except God be with him" (John 3:2). These people knew that God had approved of Him because of the power He demonstrated. Then Peter told them concerning Jesus, "You have taken by lawless hands, have crucified and put to death." (v. 23) The "lawless hands" means that they were not under the Law of Moses, that is, they were Romans who did this. But he says, "Death couldn't hold Him." He was raised from the dead on the third day; and this was a fulfillment of prophecy. Again, he points out a prophecy beginning in verse 25. David says concerning Him,

> "I foresaw the Lord always before my face,
> For He is at my right hand, that I may not be shaken.
> Therefore, my heart rejoiced, and my tongue was glad;
> Moreover, my flesh also will rest in hope.
> For You will not leave my soul in Hades,
> Nor will You allow Your Holy One to see corruption.
> You have made known to me the ways of life;
> You will make me full of joy in Your presence.'"
> **Acts 2:25-28**

He goes on to tell them that David wasn't writing this about himself. We know that because he died and because his grave is with us to this day; but it was about Jesus who died came back to life again, and he says, "We are witnesses of these things." In other words, all of us that you see with a flame of fire on our heads saw Him when He came back to life again. Luke then says a little bit later that with many other words, he testified and exhorted them to turn away from that perverse generation. No doubt he reminded them of the fact that there were over 500 different people who saw Him after He arose. This doesn't give his complete sermon that day, and by the way, let me point this out to you, this may have been another miracle. With thousands upon thousands of people gathered in the temple, some of them may have been as much as a block and a half away, and when he began to speak. They grew silent, and the ones in the farthest reaches of the crowd could hear him as he proclaimed the marvelous works of God. Now there were some of them in that crowd who believed him. They realized that he was telling the truth; and they cried out, "Men and brethren, what shall we do?" They were brokenhearted to realize that they had been complicit in the crucifixion of Jesus. But God had raised Him from the dead and made Him both Lord and Christ. He is Christ, the promised Messiah, and God has made Him Lord over all. When they heard this, they were greatly distressed; and they asked, "What can we do?" Peter's answer was, "Repent and be baptized every one of you in the name of Jesus Christ for the remission of your sins and you shall receive the gift of the Holy Spirit" (Acts 2:38 KJV). This is how you call on the name of the Lord. He was explaining to them that this is the salvation offered to those who call on the name of the Lord. This is how you claim it.

Acts 22:16 makes it very plain. It's about Saul of Tarsus. Saul was on the road to Damascus. There he saw Jesus. A bright light shone down on him that was brighter than the noonday sun. He fell to the ground; and he heard the voice of Jesus speaking to him. The light was so bright that it blinded him. He felt horrible because he thought he was serving God, and came to find out he was fighting against God. (See Acts 22:1-16) They led him by the hand into Damascus where he stayed at the home of a man named Judas on Straight Street.

If you were to go to Damascus today, you could see Straight Street. Ancient cities had very narrow winding streets. To find one that was straight was a novelty; so, they called it Straight Street. You could go to Damascus to see it today, but I recommend you look it up on the internet. It would be safer. You could see a picture of it. That street still exists. Saul went to the home of Judas on Straight Street; and for three days he fasted and prayed (Acts 9:9). He was broken-hearted because he had been fighting against the Lord. The Lord sent a man named Ananias to him; and he talked to Saul about Jesus. He said, "Why do you wait? Arise and be baptized and wash away your sins calling on the name of the Lord" (Acts 22:16). Now, this is how you surrender to the Lord. You surrender your will to His will and allow yourself to be baptized. All the while calling on the name of the Lord. He will wash away your sins and give you the gift of the Holy Spirit. Now those who gladly received His word on Pentecost responded by repenting, and all of them were baptized, 3,000 of them.

If you read the writings of people from all different denominations, you will see that everybody agrees that in the beginning, all were baptized by immersion. It changed later on, but in the beginning they were all baptized by immersion. Do you wonder how in the world they could immerse 3,000 people in one day? Let me tell you, I calculated it. I figured it out. If I were standing in water up to my chest and there was a whole long line of people coming to be baptized, I could baptize one every minute. It wouldn't take long to dip somebody in the water. About one every minute. That means 60 in an hour, and in five hours, I could baptize 300 if I could hold out. There were 12 Apostles, so 12 x 300 is 3,600. But I don't think they did it that way, because there is absolutely nothing in the New Testament that suggests you have to have certain credentials to be able to baptize somebody. I think they began by baptizing each other. It sounds novel that the Apostles baptized each other but we know from chapter 19 of Acts that people who had only been baptized with the baptism of John the Baptist were re-baptized in the name of Jesus. So, I think the Apostles started by baptizing each other; and then maybe they baptized Lazarus and asked him to help. So, they just baptized a lot of people; and those people began baptizing others; and it didn't take long to baptize 3,000 people. There were several pools in different locations throughout Jerusalem where there was enough water to allow them to go down into them and baptize people. I think that's the way it happened. However they did it, we know that they baptized 3,000 people that day. They became followers of Jesus Christ; and then it says that those who became followers of Jesus continued steadfastly in the Apostles' doctrine and in fellowship, breaking of bread and in prayers. (Acts 2:42) The "Apostles' doctrine" means the teachings of the Apostles. Jesus said that the Holy Spirit would bring all things to their remembrance. These people, who had now become followers of Jesus, were anxious to know more about Him, more about the will of God. They were anxious to hear what the Apostles were preaching and teaching. So, every day they were involved in studying God's will. They were like sponges. They couldn't soak it up fast enough.

It says they continued steadfastly in the Apostle's doctrine and in fellowship. I cannot imagine how great that fellowship was. You think about 3,000 people and every single one of them was excited about having come to know salvation through Jesus. They wanted to talk about it. That's what they wanted to talk about all the time. They talked to each other. They talked to their friends. They talked to everybody. It was so exciting. Their sins had been washed away. They had been accepted into the family of God; and they had a home in heaven. That was exciting. Has it become "old hat" to us? We've known it for so long that it's just something we don't think about that much. They thought about it. It was tremendously exciting; and they shared it with everybody.

It says they continued steadfastly in the breaking of bread. I think that primarily refers to the Lord's Supper. But I really believe that these first Christians, when they were instructed in the keeping of the Lord's Supper, realized that the bread represented the body of Jesus and the cup represented His blood. I think every time they sat down at the table, they thought about Jesus. Just couldn't help it. When they broke bread, they thought about Jesus. When they drank wine, the grape juice, they thought about Jesus. In fact, nearly everything made them think about Jesus. They were excited about it. Later, we know that they observed the Lord's Supper once every week. I think, even then, those who were close to Him, when they sat down to a meal and broke bread, they thought about Jesus. It would be great if we did that every time we sit down. Every time we pick up a piece of bread, we think about Jesus. That's the way it ought to be.

It says they continued steadfastly in prayer. Don't you know they had some amazing prayer meetings? People were so thrilled with being followers of Jesus. They knew He had ripped open the veil, opened up the Holy of Holies for them to have access to the Father. Their prayers must have been something to hear.

The chapter concludes by saying that the Lord added to their number daily those who were being saved. Don't you know people were being saved every day? Because once again, 3,000 people were talking about it. They talked to their friends. They talked to their relatives. They talked to their loved ones. They talked to everybody about Jesus. Many of them believed. People were being converted every single day. In fact, Acts tells us that a little while later, the number had grown to 5,000 men besides the women and young people. Then we read that a great company of the priests were obedient to the faith. I do not doubt that there were 15 or 20 thousand followers of Jesus in Jerusalem in a short time. It's no wonder His enemies became alarmed and tried to stamp it out. The day of Pentecost following the resurrection of Christ was one of the most exciting days in the history of the world. For the first time that day, people came to know Jesus as their Savior.

We should be as excited about it today. We should want to share that news with others. It should never become old hat to us. We've thought about it so much. Has it lost its excitement? We ought to be excited about knowing Jesus and the salvation He offers.

Discussion Questions
Chapter 2

1. What do you think convinced the people that the message of the apostles came from God?

2. How could all of the people hear Peter speak? Did the other apostles also preach that day?

3. Was the fact that all the people heard them speak in their own dialect a miracle of speaking or hearing? Did the apostles all speak in the same language and did God cause the people to hear their language? Or did they speak all those languages?

4. Do you agree that there were many people in that crowd who had been healed by Jesus?

5. How could there have been fellowship and breaking of bread when there were so many people? Do you think they met in small groups in their homes? Did they meet in the temple?

6. Did the apostles preach in the temple every day? Do you think they met in homes all over the city and the surrounding villages?

Chapter 3

Healing a Lame Man

"Now Peter and John went up together to the temple at the hour of prayer, the ninth hour. And a certain man lame from his mother's womb was carried, whom they laid daily at the gate of the temple which is called Beautiful, to ask alms from those who entered the temple; who, seeing Peter and John about to go into the temple, asked for alms. And fixing his eyes on him, with John, Peter said, "Look at us." So, he gave them his attention, expecting to receive something from them. Then Peter said, 'Silver and gold I do not have, but what I do have I give you: In the name of Jesus Christ of Nazareth, rise and walk.' And he took him by the right hand and lifted him, and immediately his feet and ankle bones received strength. So, he, leaping up, stood and walked and entered the temple with them—walking, leaping, and praising God. And all the people saw him walking and praising God. Then they knew that it was he who sat begging alms at the Beautiful Gate of the temple; and they were filled with wonder and amazement at what had happened to him." **Acts 3:1-10**

It was about 3:00 in the afternoon and in ancient Jerusalem; it was the afternoon Hour of Prayer. They had two of them. One at about 9 a.m. and one about 3 p.m. I know it's hard for us to imagine living in a society that does not live at the hectic pace we follow every day. But they did not think it strange, somehow, to take an hour out every morning to go to the temple to pray and then take another hour out of every afternoon to do the same thing.

In the temple, the priest would be preparing the daily burnt offering. In the afternoon there was the second one for the day. The burnt offering was somewhat different from the other offerings that were brought to the Lord. In the other offerings, the man who brought the sacrifice presented it to the priests, and they prepared it for the sacrifice. They removed only a certain portion of the animal, fatty portions, which they offered up on the altar. The rest of the animal was prepared as a feast to be enjoyed by the man, his family, and friends. But in the case of the burnt offering, it was called the whole burnt offering because the whole animal was prepared and placed on the altar where the whole animal was consumed by the fire. The idea of the whole burnt offering was to express to God one's desire to give himself completely without reservation, body, soul, and spirit to the service of the Lord.

When it was offered up for the nation as it was every morning and every evening at the hours of prayer, it was to indicate that the nation of Israel was dedicating itself without reservation to the God of their fathers, the God of Abraham, the God of Isaac, the God of Jacob, the God Who had brought them out of bondage in Egypt, Who had brought them safely through the Red Sea to Mt. Sinai where He gave them His law; and they became His people. A nation, no longer a mob of slaves. Now transformed into a nation. God's own chosen people. The devout from all over Jerusalem came to the temple at the hour of prayer.

In addition to the burnt offering, another priest would remove certain hot coals from the altar and place them into a golden censor. He would enter the Holy Place in the temple building. In his other hand he had powdered incense. He made the long trip from the entrance down to the other end of the Holy Place, and there, before the veil that separated the Holy Place from the Most Holy Place, was the golden altar of incense. He would dump out the hot coals onto the altar and then sprinkle the powdered incense on top of them. The smoke that went up from that incense to the ceiling, some 90 feet overhead, represented the prayers of the people going up to God. Outside of the temple in what is called the Court of Israel, the men of Israel gathered to pray. Beyond that was the Court of Women, where the women gathered, and beyond that the Court of Gentiles. The simple fact is that devout people from all over Israel came to the temple for the Hour of Prayer.

On that particular day, Peter and John were among them. I have a feeling that they were going to the temple at that particular time because there would be crowds there; and they would have an opportunity to address the crowds and talk to them about Jesus. Off to the side of the beautiful gate of the temple a beggar lay asking alms from the worshippers. This is the gate that the people liked to use most of all. It was approached by a long stairway of white marble. It had a double gate that led to a corridor that went through the temple wall into the courtyard inside. That corridor was lined with gleaming white marble. It must have been very beautiful. People liked to use that gate because of its beauty and its advantageous location. It was also a perfect place for a beggar to be placed outside of the temple, because people were going in constantly, and these were devout people, the ones who were most likely to be compassionate.

Certainly, there were those among them who had a Pharisaical attitude, who looked down their noses at anybody they considered not as good as they were. But there were among them many who were truly compassionate, who were living by that law from the Old Testament that says, "You shall love your neighbor as you love yourself." So, they would drop coins into his hand or into the receptacle he had to receive their coins.

You know it had to be a terrible experience for that beggar. He had no other way to get money for food and other necessities. There were no jobs for cripples in Jerusalem at that time. He was a beggar, not because he wanted to be, but because he had no other choice. He had no way to make a living. It was degrading and debasing; and he must have felt terrible with no self-esteem whatsoever. Most people didn't even look at him as they passed by. I know that because I've seen human nature; and I know people don't want to look at a beggar. They're embarrassed by him. But occasionally someone would stop and drop a coin into his hand. When he saw Peter and John about to enter, he asked alms from them; and they stopped, which was unusual, and they looked at him. Again, that was unusual because people didn't ordinarily look him in the eye. Then they said, "Look at us." He expected to receive something from them. Peter said to him, "Silver and gold I do not have, but what I do have I give you: In the name of Jesus Christ of Nazareth, rise and walk" (Acts 4:6).

Then he reached down and took him by the hand and helped him to his feet; and the man felt something that he had never felt before in his life. He felt strength in his feet and his ankle bones; and he realized that he was standing on his own. He took a tentative step and then another; and then he realized he was walking, and somewhere along about that time, I think he thought, "I wonder if I could jump?" So, he tried to jump; and it worked. I cannot imagine the excitement on his face and the joy that was expressed as he grabbed hold of Peter and John and went into the temple with them, shouting his praises to the Lord. I think he began to shout, "I can walk! I can walk! Look at this, I can jump. Praise God!" Such was his excitement that people were drawn to him. They ran to Peter and John to see what in the world was going on.

I want us to stop and think for a moment about what happened to the beggar that day. His life was totally transformed. Now you think about it. He had never been able to work. I'm sure he was not married. Who in the world would marry a beggar? Who in the world would a beggar ask to marry him? But now he could get a job. He could have some dignity. He could have some self-respect, and perhaps he could get married; and he could become a father. His life was truly transformed by the gift he received from God that day. Let me ask you something. Has your life ever been transformed by a gift from God? I bet everyone reading this could say, "Yes." For every one of us, the day we met the Lord and decided to give our lives to Him was a transforming day.

A transforming day in my life also occurred when the Navy sent me to Memphis, Tennessee. I went there to study electronics to become an Aviation Electronics Technician. While I was there, I discovered that a new Bible College called Memphis Christian College had just been started. I knew I wanted to go to Bible College. So, I requested permanent duty in Memphis; and the Navy, by the grace of God, gave me permanent duty there. I began my permanent duty in May of 1960, and in August of 1960, I joined the workforce that worked at night. Then in September, I began going to Bible College in the daytime. I was able to complete about a year and a half of college during my last two years in the Navy, because God gave me the blessing of arranging for me to stay in Memphis.

He also allowed me to fall in love with the South. I was raised in Indiana; and after I had been in the South for a while, I didn't want to go back. I tell people that I am an American by birth and a Southerner by the grace of God. It took me six years to get my degree from Memphis Christian College because I could only go to school part-time. About two years before I got my degree, Diane showed up at Memphis Christian College; and we got together. Now we have been together for more than 50 years. It was truly life-changing.

I'm sure many of you could tell similar stories about how your life has been changed, maybe when you got married. Maybe when your first child was born. Maybe when you began a job that turned out to be your career. There have been life-changing moments that came because God is in charge. You know that's what it is. The Navy thought they were assigning me that duty there in Memphis, but they didn't know that God was in charge. If you stop and think about it, you will see that the Apostles had a wonderful opportunity that day. The Holy Spirit directed them to heal this man. God used them to be life-changing for him.

I can't help but wonder. Maybe we knew it. Maybe we didn't know it. Maybe we have said or done something that made a major change in someone's life. Several years ago, when I was a young preacher, I was preaching at church in Mississippi. There was a young man who had finished high school and gone on to college at the University. He came home after his first year in college, and I invited him to work with us in church camp for a week; and he agreed to do it. During that week, God gave him a gift. He showed him that there is great joy in serving the Lord. So, in September, instead of going back to the University, he went to Eastern Christian College to learn to be a preacher. While there, he met a lovely young lady who became his wife. His life was transformed by the gift of joy and by the grace of God.

That's what Peter and John did that day. They seized the opportunity. When this man grabbed them and held on and began to shout about how he had been healed. People began to run together; and a great crowd formed. Peter took the opportunity to talk to them about Jesus. That's an important idea. When the opportunity arises, we must seize it.

Let me tell you another personal story. Diane and I were out visiting one night. We had gone out to see a family that someone had said might be interested in our church. When we got to their home, no one was there. So, we headed back home. We didn't have any other place that we had planned to go. We were passing by the home of one of our church members and remembered that he had just told us that he had a new neighbor who had moved in next door. We thought we would stop there and invite them to church. So, we pulled into their driveway, walked into the carport and knocked on the door. A young lady came to the door. She was crying. Her little boy had been sick that day and hadn't been able to keep any fluids down; and they had heard from their doctor that when dehydration might be a problem, you can check by grabbing the skin on the back of the hand, and if it pops back into place immediately, it's good. If you are as old as I am, it doesn't pop back immediately. It takes a while. But with a child, it pops back immediately. They had tried that with their little boy; and it hadn't popped back immediately. They realized that he was becoming dehydrated. Her husband was on the phone with the doctor at that moment. He said, "You need to get him to the emergency room."

Surprisingly, under the circumstances, the young lady invited us in; and Diane went with her to the other room to prepare the diaper bag and whatever else she needed to prepare to take the baby to the hospital. When they were ready to go, we paused for just a moment to have a prayer with them. God put us in that place at that time. The timing was perfect. As a result, I had the privilege of baptizing that young man. He and his wife moved their membership; and they became faithful members of the church and our good friends.

When the opportunity arises, we need to seize it for Jesus. When the Apostle Peter had the opportunity that day, he preached to them about Jesus. Let me share with you some of what he had to say. Beginning at verse 12 of chapter 3, the Apostle Peter said this, "Men of Israel, why do you marvel at this, or why look so intently at us as though by our own power or godliness we had made this man walk? The God of Abraham, Isaac, and Jacob, the God of our fathers, glorified his servant Jesus, whom you delivered up and denied in the presence of Pilate when he was determined to let him go. But you denied the Holy One and the Just and asked that a murderer be granted to you and killed the Prince of Life, whom God raised from the dead, of which we are witnesses." You see what he did? The very first thing he did was turn their minds away from themselves and focus their attention on Jesus. Jesus was the source of the blessing. They made sure that the people understood that He was the source of the blessing; and then Peter pointed out to them that they had taken this One that God had glorified and had been responsible for His death. Now, chances are that most of the people in that crowd that day were not in the crowd that was clamoring for His crucifixion. It happened very early in the morning. It was about six o'clock in the morning when they took Him to Pilate for trial, and most of them probably had not heard about it, but by the time they led Him up the Trail of Sorrows to Mount Calvary, it was about nine o'clock in the morning. I'm sure the word had spread throughout Jerusalem, and they could have stood up for him if they had wanted to. On the day of the Triumphal Entry, there were thousands, if not hundreds of thousands, of people who were proclaiming Him the Messiah when they cried out, "Hosanna to the King who comes in the name of the Lord!" Had those same people stood up for Jesus, there is no way the Romans would have executed Him that day. So, they were complicit even though they were not directly involved. They were complicit in the death of the Savior.

It's interesting to me that He did not tell them that they were a part of a depraved race who had inherited guilt from Adam. He told them about their own specific sins that had condemned them. Then he told them what they needed to do to be saved. He said to them, in verses 16-19, "And His name through faith in His name has made this man strong whom you see and know. Yes, and the faith which comes through Him has given him this perfect soundness in the presence of you all. Yet now, brethren, I know that you did it in ignorance, as did also your rulers. But those things which God foretold by the mouth of all His prophets, that the Christ would suffer, He has thus fulfilled. Repent therefore and be converted, that your sins may be blotted out, so that times of refreshing may come from the presence of the Lord." This is a parallel passage to the one in the second chapter where he says, "Repent and be baptized for the remission of sins and you will receive the gift of the Holy Spirit." It's another way of stating the same thing. He is saying, "Repent and turn. Turn to God." The way you turn to God is by surrendering your will to His will and by being baptized. Then your sins will be washed away; and you will receive the gift of the Holy Spirit. Peter turned their attention away from himself and John to Jesus. He showed them that they were guilty of sin and needed a savior. Then he told them what they needed to do to be saved. If we want to talk to people about their salvation, that's the thing we need to do. We need to be humble. It's not our ability to save. It's His ability to save. We need to tell them to focus on Jesus; and then show them what they need to do in order to lay claim to the salvation He offers.

Discussion Questions
Chapter 3

1. Have you ever encountered a beggar? Did you look him or her in the eye?

2. What does it tell you about his healing when he was able to walk and leap? Wouldn't you expect him to need some time to develop the ability to run and leap?

3. Do you think God puts us in certain places at just the right time to witness about our faith? Can you tell a story of such a time in your life?

4. Would you be willing to baptize someone who wanted to become a Christian?

5. Do you think there are people in America today who make a living through begging?

Chapter 4

A Prayer for Boldness

"And being let go, they went to their own companions and reported all that the chief priests and elders had said to them. So, when they heard that, they raised their voice to God with one accord and said: 'Lord, You are God, who made heaven and earth and the sea, and all that is in them, who by the mouth of Your servant David have said:

"Why did the nations rage,
And the people plot vain things?
The kings of the earth took their stand,
And the rulers were gathered together
Against the Lord and against His Christ."

'For truly against Your holy Servant Jesus, whom You anointed, both Herod and Pontius Pilate, with the Gentiles and the people of Israel, were gathered together to do whatever Your hand and Your purpose determined before to be done. Now, Lord, look on their threats, and grant to Your servants that with all boldness they may speak Your word, by stretching out Your hand to heal, and that signs and wonders may be done through the name of Your holy Servant Jesus.'"

And when they had prayed, the place where they were assembled was shaken; and they were all filled with the Holy Spirit, and they spoke the word of God with boldness.

Now the multitude of those who believed were of one heart and one soul; neither did anyone say that any of the things he possessed was his own, but they had all things in common. And with great power the apostles gave witness to the resurrection of the Lord Jesus. And great grace was upon them all. Nor was there anyone among them who lacked; for all who were possessors of lands or houses sold them, and brought the proceeds of the things that were sold, and laid them at the apostles' feet; and they distributed to each as anyone had need.

And Joses, who was also named Barnabas by the apostles (which is translated Son of Encouragement), a Levite of the country of Cyprus, having land, sold it, and brought the money and laid it at the apostles' feet."

Acts 4:23-37

The first great wave of persecution that washed over the church began with the arrest of the apostles Peter and John following the healing of the lame man at the beautiful gate of the temple. Let me remind you of what happened. Peter and John were going into the temple for the afternoon hour of prayer. They were entering through the beautiful gate of the temple; and they encountered a lame man who had been laid there by the side of the gate by his friends. He was asking for alms. Peter looked at him and said, "Silver and gold I do not have, but what I do have, I give you: In the name of Jesus Christ of Nazareth, rise and walk." Then he reached out, took him by the hand, and helped him to his feet. The man felt something he had never felt before. He felt strength in his feet and ankles. He discovered he could walk; and the Bible says he began walking, leaping, and praising God. I am sure he was shouting his praises, so people began to gather round to see what the commotion was all about. No doubt many of them recognized him as the beggar who lay by the gate every day asking for alms. Here he was walking and leaping and praising God; and he grabbed Peter and John. He held onto them until a large crowd gathered around. Of course, Peter and John had no intention of leaving. This was an opportunity they were glad to have.

As soon as the crowd had gathered, Peter began to preach to them about Jesus. As a result of that incident, a great many more people were added to the company of believers, the church. The Bible does not tell us how many became Christians that day, but when the fourth chapter of Acts opens, it tells us in verse four that the number of men who became a part of the church increased to about 5,000. The 3,000 became perhaps 10 or 15 thousand when you include women and young people. This was all in Jerusalem. As a result, the religious leaders of the Jews became alarmed. They were almost in a panic mode. You can understand why. In a city about the size of Birmingham, Alabama, in just a few days about 15,000 people became followers of this new religion. Everywhere they went, they were talking about it. They were talking to their families. They were talking to their friends. They were talking to anyone who would listen. They were excited about it. They were talking about Jesus and how God, through Him, had provided salvation, forgiveness for their sins, and the promise of a home in heaven for eternity. Within a few days, everyone in Jerusalem knew something was happening. The religious leaders realized that if this continued, it wouldn't be long before a majority of the people in Jerusalem would be following Jesus; and it would spread throughout the country until no one was following them anymore. They would lose their position and their power and their source of wealth.

They decided they had to do something to stop it, so they sent out the temple guard, the police force, to arrest Peter and John. They brought them in, locked them up for the night, and brought them before the council the next day. It's very interesting to see what happened because they didn't have any charges against them. Would they charge them with healing without a license? In addition, the man they healed was there to testify on their behalf.

We don't know if the council called him or if he appeared on his own. He was standing there with them. This man, who had never taken a step in forty years of life, was now walking and was standing with Peter and John.

The council decided to ask them a vague question, hoping they would incriminate themselves. They thought these were uneducated men who would be ill-equipped to speak for themselves. So, they asked, "By what power or by what name have you done this?" They might very well have said, "Done what?" But they didn't. Peter jumped right into the middle of the problem.

"Then Peter, filled with the Holy Spirit, said to them, 'Rulers of the people and elders of Israel: If we this day are judged for a good deed done to a helpless man, by what means he has been made well, let it be known to you all, and to all the people of Israel, that by the name of Jesus Christ of Nazareth, whom you crucified, whom God raised from the dead, by Him this man stands here before you whole. This is the stone which was rejected by you builders, which has become the chief cornerstone. Nor is there salvation in any other, for there is no other name under heaven given among men by which we must be saved'" (Acts 4:8-12).

Did you get that? He said, "If we are being judged for the good deed done to this man, then let it be known that it was done in the name of Jesus, whom you crucified and whom God has raised from the dead." He boldly proclaimed what they wanted to stamp out; and because the man they healed was standing there with them, there was nothing they could say. The council took note of the fact that these men had been with Jesus. The thing that must have astonished them was that these same men had gone into hiding after Jesus was crucified. Now they were boldly proclaiming that it was through His power that this miracle was possible. They thought this transformation from cowering in fear to standing boldly and proclaiming their faith in Jesus was unbelievable. There wasn't even a hint of fear in them.

They put them out of the council meeting and conferred among themselves about what to do. They decided they would severely threaten them and command them to stop preaching in His name. The response of the apostles was magnificent. "Peter and John answered and said to them, 'Whether it is right in the sight of God to listen to you more than to God, you judge. For we cannot but speak the things which we have seen and heard.'"

The council must have been seething with anger, but there was nothing more they could do, so they threatened them again and let them go. So, they went back to their companions, the other apostles, their friends, and others who were also followers of Jesus, and reported what had transpired in the council. When they heard their report, they responded by joining together in prayer. There was no whining. No one complained. They prayed and said. I'm paraphrasing here. They said, "Lord, this is just what you said would happen. There are powerful forces arrayed against us, so give us boldness that we may speak Your word; and stretch out Your hand with healing and signs and wonders done in the name of Jesus."

Now, that's the kind of prayer God is pleased to answer. When their prayer ended, the place where they were meeting together was shaken, and they were all filled with the Holy Spirit, and they did not cease preaching and teaching in the name of Jesus.

That's the kind of prayer we need to pray. We are facing tremendous forces that are arrayed against us. The media, academia, the entertainment industry, and government are opposing the clear teaching of the word of

God. We do not need to whine and complain about it. We need to pray, "Oh God, make us bold to take a stand for our faith." It would be good for us to wear sweatshirts that proclaim our faith. They could say things like, "I stand with Jesus!" and "Jesus is the King," and many others. Let us boldly proclaim the gospel. Let us not be ashamed or timid. We need to go forth without fear. We need to remember that the blood of martyrs is the fuel that feeds the flame of revival.

There are very few churches in the history of Christianity that could be called truly great churches. The church in Jerusalem at that time was one of them. There are several reasons why it could be called great.

It was a great church because it had great leaders. At this time all twelve apostles were working with and leading them. We know that Jesus had promised them that the Holy Spirit would be with them and lead them to all truth. He would enable them to remember all He had taught them. We know that the apostles were teaching everything the Holy Spirit directed them to teach. The people in that church were receiving the pure word of God from the mouths of the apostles every day. There was no dilution, no alteration, no changes. They were receiving the truth from God. The leaders of that church were totally dedicated, sold out for Jesus. There is no reason why we can't have that kind of leadership in our churches today. Those of us who lead should pray, "Lord, You are the Potter, I am the clay. Make me what you want me to be." We have the same Gospel they had right here in the Bible. We need to study it diligently. Memorize it. Make sure our hearts are filled with it. There is no reason why we can't teach the truth just like they did. It is our responsibility to pray and seek His face. We can go forward in the strength He gives us.

The church in Jerusalem was great because it attracted huge numbers of people to Jesus. But it is not enough to attract a great many people. We could fill our churches every week. It could be standing room only, but if lives are not being transformed into the image of Christ, it is not a great church. If people are not being transformed, we are not doing the job. We are missing the mark. The church in Jerusalem was great because it brought in huge numbers of people, and those people were being transformed. How do I know they were being transformed? The scripture says, in verse 32 of this chapter, "The multitude of those who believed were of one heart and of one soul." They were united!

There was no difference between the teachings of one apostle and the others. They all taught the same truth. It also says that none of the people considered the things they owned as belonging to themselves. It all belonged to God; and if it was needed by anyone, they were willing to give it. "Nor was there anyone among them who lacked; for all who were possessors of lands or houses sold them, and brought the proceeds of the things that were sold, and laid them at the apostles' feet; and they distributed to each as anyone had need" (Acts 4:34-35).

No one coerced them to do it. They did it because God had transformed their hearts. They loved their neighbors as themselves. Those offerings were used to support those who could not support themselves, principally the widows. They gave willingly and wanted no credit for it.

Let me tell you something. You know the expression, "Blood is thicker than water?" Do you know the origin of that saying? The water it speaks of is the water of baptism. The expression means, "The ties between blood relatives are stronger than those formed by the church." It's not true! The ties between brothers and sisters in the church are stronger than those in families. I have many brothers and sisters in the Lord who are just as dear to me as the other children born to my mother and father. We must love one another. The Bible says, "Beloved, let us love one another, for love is of God; and everyone who loves is born of God and knows God. He who does not love does not know God, for God is love" (1 John 4:7-8). The church at Jerusalem was great because they loved one another; and they expressed their love by giving. Love is always expressed by giving. We want the ones we love to always have the best. We express our love by giving ourselves. We give our time to those we love. Our children want our time more than anything else because they know instinctively that you love them when you give them your time.

Discussion Questions
Chapter 4

1. If you were arrested for proclaiming your faith, would you continue preaching when they threatened you?

2. Why were they willing to face prison or death rather than renounce their faith?

3. If you were in that situation, would you pray that they would see the light and stop the persecution? Or would you pray for courage to keep witnessing for Jesus? Both?

4. Do any of us pray for the terrorists who bomb Israel? Jesus said we should pray for those who spitefully use us and persecute us. Do we?

5. If our leaders set this kind of example, would we follow?

Chapter 5

Ananias and Sapphira

"But when the officers came and did not find them in the prison, they returned and reported, saying, 'Indeed we found the prison shut securely, and the guards standing outside before the doors; but when we opened them, we found no one inside!' Now when the high priest, the captain of the temple, and the chief priests heard these things, they wondered what the outcome would be. So, one came and told them, saying, 'Look, the men whom you put in prison are standing in the temple and teaching the people!

Then the captain went with the officers and brought them without violence, for they feared the people, lest they should be stoned. And when they had brought them, they set them before the council. And the high priest asked them, saying, 'Did we not strictly command you not to teach in this name? And look, you have filled Jerusalem with your doctrine, and intend to bring this Man's blood on us!'

But Peter and the other apostles answered and said: 'We ought to obey God rather than men. The God of our fathers raised up Jesus whom you murdered by hanging on a tree. Him God has exalted to His right hand to be Prince and Savior, to give repentance to Israel and forgiveness of sins. And we are His witnesses to these things, and so also is the Holy Spirit whom God has given to those who obey Him.'

When they heard this, they were furious and plotted to kill them."

Acts 5:22-33

The fifth chapter of Acts tells the story of some problems that arose in the church, problems that arose from inside and problems that came from outside. It also tells about how the Holy Spirit led them to solve those problems positively. So, the reputation of the church was elevated, a great many souls came to know the Lord, and the name of the Lord was glorified. If we want to know how to handle problems in the church, we should study this chapter and the next one.

The first problem that arose in chapter five had to do with a couple named Ananias and Sapphira. The problem began because of an attitude that was generally shared by the people in the church in Jerusalem. When the scripture says that "They were all of one mind and one heart," it does not mean that every single person in the church felt that way. When you are talking about a group of several thousand, you are not going to have every single one of them thinking the same way. In general, you could say they agreed. The vast majority of them thought the same way. The attitude I'm talking about said, "Nothing I possess is my own. It all belongs to God." Some of the Christians had property they weren't using, and they felt moved to sell it and give the money to the apostles to use in helping the widows and the poorest among them. No one required them to do that. It was not something the whole church did. All of them didn't sell their property and pooled it and distribute to all to meet their needs. This was not an early experiment in communism. Everyone was able to retain their own possessions. When people did sell property and give the proceeds to the apostles, they did it because their own compassion compelled them to do all they could to help. They also did it to please the Lord.

They didn't all do it. In fact, many of those who were wealthy kept their property and dedicated it to the Lord. They made it available for the church to use in any way they could. A case in point is Mary, the mother of John

Mark. This is the Mark who wrote the gospel of Mark. His mother owned a large house in Jerusalem. She made that house available for the church to use. Acts 12:1-17 tells the story of Peter being arrested by Herod. In the middle of the night, an angel set him free. He went to the home of Mary, where a large number of Christians had gathered to pray for him. The fact that he knew how to go to her house is evidence that it was a meeting place they often used. You see what I am getting at. There were people in the church who had property that they kept but dedicated to the Lord.

This attitude is what is important, Whatever I possess is not mine. It belongs to the Lord. If it can be used in any way for His glory, it is available. If my house is needed to show hospitality to a visiting missionary, it is available. If it is needed to host a Bible study group, it is available. The same thing is true of our cars. If my car can be used to take someone to the hospital, it is available. It belongs to the Lord, and He can use it in any way He wants to. That was the attitude of the people in the church in Jerusalem. Some of them, like Barnabas, sold their property and gave the money to the apostles to use for the relief of the widows and others who needed assistance. When they did that, a great many people in the church praised them for their generosity. That is the very reason Jesus told us that when we give, it should be in secret. Your right hand should not know what your left hand is doing. We are not to give to be praised by men, but to benefit others and to please the Lord. He who sees in secret will reward you openly.

When Ananias and Sapphira saw how those people were being praised for their generosity, they wanted some of that for themselves. They decided to give, not because they had generous hearts, but because they wanted to be praised. So, they sold a piece of property, gave part of the proceeds to the apostles, and kept some for themselves. They had a perfect right to do that. The apostle Peter told Ananias that while he had the property, it was his to do with whatever he wanted; and after he sold it, the money was his. If he wanted to keep it all, that was his decision. The problem was that they gave part of the proceeds of the sale and said it was the whole amount. In other words, they lied about it. Peter confronted Ananias about the gift. He said, "Ananias, why has Satan filled your heart to lie to the Holy Spirit and keep back part of the price of the land for yourself?" Then he added, "You have not lied to men but to God." (Acts 5:3, 4) Ananias dropped dead at the feet of Peter. As you would expect, great fear came upon everyone who heard about it. Some young men came in and took his body out and buried it.

About three hours later Sapphira came in not knowing about what had happened. It seems amazing that no one had told her about Ananias. Peter asked her about the price they got for the land. She indicated it was as her husband had said. So, Peter said to her, "How is it that you have agreed together to test the Spirit of the Lord? Look, the feet of those who have buried your husband are at the door, and they will carry you out" (Acts 5:9). Immediately, she fell dead. The young men came in and carried her body out and buried it beside her husband.

Great fear came upon the church. They were in awe, realizing that God was in their midst. It was obvious to everyone that no human hand was involved in the death of Ananias and Sapphira. God struck them down. So not only people inside the church, but also those outside the church got the idea that God was in the midst of these people.

When thousands of them gathered together in the temple, no one joined them unless he was perfectly sincere in his desire to follow Jesus. The people realized it didn't pay to be hypocritical before the Lord.

Now you might wonder, as I have, "Why did God deal so harshly with this couple?" The same kind of hypocrisy happens frequently in the church today; and He doesn't punish these hypocrites like He did those. People lie about what they give to the church. They used to lie about it on their income tax forms, but the government has cracked down on that.

This is what I believe is the answer. Throughout the Bible, the first time a particular sin occurs, God deals with it very harshly to make it very plain what He thinks about it. That is what happened to Sodom and Gomorrah. So far as we know, that was the first time in the history of the world when there was widespread practice of homosexuality that was accepted in a particular location. God showed what He thought about it when He rained fire and brimstone on those cities so that they were utterly destroyed. Now, He expects us to understand that. There won't be any fire and brimstone raining down, but those who practice that evil will meet with another fire when they come to stand before the Lord.

When the Lord shows through a dramatic demonstration what He thinks about a matter, He expects us to take notice. That's what He did with Ananias and Sapphira. Now he expects us to understand how He feels about that.

James talked about our language in chapter three of his book. He said in verses 8 through 10, "But no man can tame the tongue. It is an unruly evil, full of deadly poison. With it we bless our God and Father, and with it we curse men, who have been made in the similitude of God. Out of the same mouth proceed blessing and cursing. My brethren, these things ought not to be so." He talked about the fact that you can't get salt water and fresh water from the same source. If you put salt water in there, it fouls the whole source. He is saying that the same thing is true of our speech. Poison your language with vulgar and profane words, and it pollutes all of your speech. The mouth that curses a fellow man can't then bless God. His speech is reprehensible to God, whether it is directed at Him or His children. Let me state this principle again. Throughout the scriptures, when God encounters a sin for the first time, He deals with it harshly. He doesn't continue to punish it the same way after that, but He expects us to remember what He thinks about that sin.

Here is another fact you need to understand. Although the apostles were given the ability to heal all kinds of diseases, the use of that power was directed by the Holy Spirit. Jesus could and did heal everyone who came to Him for help. There is no record of Him ever turning anyone down. But it wasn't like that for the apostles. They could only heal when the Holy Spirit prompted them. Paul wasn't able to heal himself. He spoke of his thorn in the flesh, a physical ailment. He says, "A thorn in the flesh was given to me, a messenger of Satan to buffet me, lest I be exalted above measure. Concerning this thing, I pleaded with the Lord three times that it might depart from me. And He said to me, 'My grace is sufficient for you, for My strength is made perfect in weakness.'" Paul also had a dear friend named Epaphroditus, whom he could not heal. He was afraid he was going to die. You might ask, "Why didn't he heal him?" The answer is that the Holy Spirit did not direct him to heal his friend. He says concerning him, "For indeed he was sick almost unto death; but God had mercy on him, and not only on him but on me also, lest I should have sorrow upon sorrow" (Philippians 2:27). So, he prayed for his friend and waited on the Lord just as we do.

There are two times in the book of Acts where a special season of miracles is described. One is right here in the fifth chapter in verses 15 and 16, "they brought the sick out into the streets and laid them on beds and couches, that at least the shadow of Peter passing by might fall on some of them. Also, a multitude gathered from the surrounding cities to Jerusalem, bringing sick people and those who were tormented by unclean spirits, and they were all healed." The other is in chapter 19:11-12, "Now God worked unusual miracles by the hands of Paul, so that even handkerchiefs or aprons were brought from his body to the sick, and the diseases left them and the evil spirits went out of them." As you can imagine, as a result of these special seasons of miracles, the reputation and appeal of the church grew; and many more people turned to the Lord.

Another result of the special season of miracles in Jerusalem, was the reaction of the Jewish leaders. They were afraid the whole city would turn to Christ. They thought, "We've got to do something about this." They knew their positions of power and influence were in jeopardy; and if they lost those things, the source of their wealth would also be gone.

They decided to arrest all twelve of the apostles. This was the second problem the church in Jerusalem faced. They took them into custody and locked them up for the night, but an angel of the Lord set them free and instructed them to go to the temple and speak to the people about this life in Christ. So, they did just that.

When the council convened that morning, they sent to the prison to have the apostles brought to them. You can imagine their great concern when the officers came back and told them they had found the prison locked up and the guards in front of the doors, but when they opened the doors, there was no one inside. Then someone came in and reported that the men who had been arrested were standing in the temple teaching. The council wondered where this was going. They should have thought, "It looks like God is on their side. Maybe we should be, too." But they did not think that; they thought, "How are we going to stop this?"

So, they sent the temple police to get them. They, in turn, went to the temple and asked the apostles to come to the council. The Bible says they brought them without violence because they feared the people. I think it went something like this. When they found the apostles, they asked, "Would you mind coming with us? The council wants to talk to you." So, the apostles agreed to go.

When they stood before the council the High Priest said to them, "Did we not strictly command you not to teach in this name? And look, you have filled Jerusalem with your doctrine, and intend to bring this Man's blood on us!" (Acts 5:28) Then Peter and the other apostles answered, "We ought to obey God rather than men. The God of our fathers raised up Jesus, whom you murdered by hanging on a tree. Him God has exalted to His right hand to be Prince and Savior, to give repentance to Israel and forgiveness of sins. And we are His witnesses to these things, and so also is the Holy Spirit whom God has given to those who obey Him."

The council was furious, and they plotted to kill them, but one cooler head prevailed. There was among them a noted scholar named Gamaliel. As was his right as a member of the council, he called the meeting to a halt and had the apostles ushered out of the room. Then he turned to the council and reminded them of two different men who had recently gathered a following, but when each of them was killed, their followers dispersed. Then he advised that they leave these men alone; and if this movement was from men, it would soon go away, but if it was of God, you couldn't stop it, and you wouldn't want to fight with God. The council decided to take his advice, and after beating them and threatening them again, they let them go. Then a remarkable thing happened. The apostles went on their way rejoicing that they were counted worthy to suffer for Jesus.

I've thought about that a lot. I wondered why they rejoiced. I have concluded that there were two reasons why they rejoiced. First, it was because God had confidence in them. They were glad that He was pleased with them because they endured suffering and remained faithful. They were glad He believed in them. He knew they would remain faithful; and they rejoiced because He had that confidence in them. Second, they rejoiced because their suffering put them in good company. They remembered Jesus had said, "Blessed are you when they revile and persecute you, and say all kinds of evil against you falsely for My sake. Rejoice and be exceedingly glad, for great is your reward in heaven, for so they persecuted the prophets who were before you" (Matthew 5:11-12). When they were persecuted, it put them in good company. Down through the ages, the servants of God have been persecuted by the people of the world. If you would like to know more about how Christians have suffered, you might want to check out Fox's Book of Martyrs. It is available online. I think you know, as I do, that it could be possible that you and I could be persecuted for our faith. If we are, I hope and pray our attitude will be like theirs. We will rejoice that we were counted worthy to suffer for Him.

Then the scriptures tell us that every day in the temple and from house to house, they did not cease preaching and teaching Jesus as the Christ. The beating and the threats did not slow them down one bit. I hope we will seek to emulate them in teaching about Jesus. Let us let the world know we stand with Jesus.

Discussion Questions
Chapter 5

1. Do you think Ananias and Sapphira will go to hell? Why or why not?

2. Why doesn't God punish hypocrites in the church today as He did then?

3. Do you think there were any close friends of Ananias and Sapphira who mourned for them? Would they have mourned openly? Would the church have mourned?

4. If you knew a brother or sister in Christ who was arrested, would you mourn for him or her? Would you visit him or her in prison?

Chapter 6

Deacons

"Now in those days, when the number of the disciples was multiplying, there arose a complaint against the Hebrews by the Hellenists, because their widows were neglected in the daily distribution. Then the twelve summoned the multitude of the disciples and said, 'We shouldn't leave the word of God and serve tables. Therefore, brethren, seek out from among you seven men of good reputation, full of the Holy Spirit and wisdom, whom we may appoint over this business; but we will give ourselves continually to prayer and to the ministry of the word.' And the saying pleased the whole multitude. And they chose Stephen, a man full of faith and the Holy Spirit, and Philip, Prochorus, Nicanor, Timon, Parmenas, and Nicolas, a proselyte from Antioch, whom they set before the apostles; and when they had prayed, they laid hands on them. Then the word of God spread, and the number of the disciples multiplied greatly in Jerusalem, and a great many of the priests were obedient to the faith."

Acts 6:1-7

I want to discuss Deacons in the New Testament church. Let me begin by saying that the word Deacon is a transliteration of the Greek word Diakonos. You see, they did not translate the word; they simply brought the sound of the word over into English. Diakonos became Deacon in English. The word means servant, and it is used extensively throughout the New Testament. It's used in the noun form, either "service" or "servant," and in the verb form, which is "to serve" or "serving." It is found very frequently throughout the New Testament. Sometimes it refers to men who served as deacons in the church; and sometimes it is simply talking about serving. A case in point is the passage of scripture before us here.

The reason these seven men who are chosen are called the first seven deacons is that this word is used so extensively in this passage of scripture. It's found in the first verse when it says, "there was a complaint by the Hellenist against the Hebrews because their widows were neglected in the daily distribution." The word translated "distribution" is a form of the word diakonos. In other words, the widows were being served by the church. They provided for their needs with food and other necessities. Then in verse two, where the apostles say, "we shouldn't leave the word of God to serve tables." The word translated "serve" is another instance of a form of the word diakonos. In verse four, the apostles say, "We will give ourselves continually to prayer and the ministry of the word." The word translated "ministry" is another form of the word diakonos. Their ministry, their service to the church, was in teaching the word of God.

This much we know for certain: the apostles invited the people to choose seven men from among them; and they would appoint them to serve. In other words, they would delegate authority to them to take care of this job that the church needs to be doing. They recognized from the beginning that the widows needed the support of the church; and they were distributing to them, but the apostles said, "Our job is to pray for the people and to teach the word of God. We are too busy with these responsibilities to take care of matters such as this business of distributing food to the widows."

Basically, they are saying, "We are exercising oversight in instructing you to select these men; and we will appoint them. We will lay hands on them and ordain them; and we will set them apart for the task of doing this job of distributing food and necessities to the widows." They were chosen for a specific job and were formally made servants of the church.

Sometimes in the New Testament, when it's talking about servants of the church or deacons, it's talking about those who have been formally set aside and given a job to do in service to the church. Sometimes it's talking about the simple service that we render to one another as we seek to follow the will of the Lord. Now that same program, that same way of doing things, is in effect in the church today. The church still has jobs that need to be done that the ones who are in positions of leadership don't have time to do. They teach and preach the word. They are the shepherds of the flock, who seek those who have gone astray, who lift those who are cast down, who counsel those who are in need. Those who are involved in that kind of ministry are not too good to do these things. They just don't have time. So, it is their job to appoint others who can be trusted to take care of these things. Things such as the job of the treasurer of the church. Somebody has to receive the funds, deposit them in the bank, write the checks, distribute the funds to pay for the light bill, the water bill, the maintenance of the property, the maintenance of the building itself, the cleaning, and that sort of thing. All of these kinds of things are jobs that need to be done, and somebody has to be the one who distributes the funds to get them done.

The same thing can be true in regard to other jobs. We need someone to lead the singing, somebody to pass the emblems when we have the Lord's Supper, and somebody to pass the collection plate. All of these things are jobs that need to be done; and the ones who are in the position of being shepherds caring for the flock don't need to be distracted from their study and their teaching of the word to take care of things like that. So, they have the responsibility to appoint those who are trustworthy to take care of these jobs in the church today. That's the way it should be. That's the way it was in the New Testament church. That's the way it should be today.

There are so many passages in the New Testament that use the word diakonos that we cannot even begin to examine all of them, but I want to take a look at a couple of categories in which this word was used. For example, in the 19th chapter of the book of Acts in verse 22, it talks about two men, Timothy and Erastus, who were assistants for the apostle Paul. They traveled with him; and they helped him in whatever way he needed assistance. I have an idea that one of them was the treasurer of the group. When they came into town, he was the guy who went into the marketplace and bought food for them and arranged for lodging for them. Somebody had to do those things; and Paul delegated someone to take care of those things for them. He had someone to take care of them who traveled with him. He could concentrate on his job of teaching and preaching the word of God. These two men also became his protégés. He was their mentor; and he taught them how they could carry on the work that he was doing. Later on, we see that Timothy was an evangelist. We don't read a whole lot about Erastus after this, but we know that he may have become an evangelist. Paul wrote to him when he was serving at churches in different locations. The thing that I want to point out is that the elders or the apostles and those who were in positions of teaching and being shepherds to the flock had men who worked under them who were their protégés. They were teaching and delivering the word to them that they might be prepared to give that word to others also. The apostle Paul tells them that they have that kind of responsibility.

So, these men were assistants to the apostle Paul, I feel sure that later on, he sent them ahead of his group to a place they would be going. I am assuming that when they got to town, they would find the Christians. Then they informed the elders of the local congregation that Paul was coming.

Then they got the word out to all the Christians; and they gathered the crowds together so they could be ready when Paul got there, so he could preach to them. They took care of all of those things. I'd say they handed out the flyers. They did everything they could to get the word out that the apostle Paul was coming to prepare for his arrival. So, it is appropriate today in the church that some take care of all the business matters of the church. In the church today, we not only have deacons, but we also have a treasurer, trustees, song leaders, and Sunday School teachers. There are all kinds of jobs that are being done by people who are serving the church. They may not be selected and formally set aside and ordained for the task that they are doing, but from the goodness of their hearts, they are willing to serve. That is exactly as it should be.

The other passage of scripture that I want to point out to you is Ephesians 4:11-13. "And He Himself gave some to be apostles, some prophets, some evangelists, and some pastors and teachers, for the equipping of the saints for the work of ministry, for the edifying of the body of Christ, till we all come to the unity of the faith and of the knowledge of the Son of God, to a perfect man, to the measure of the stature of the fullness of Christ." There the apostle Paul talks about the gifts God gave to the church, the leadership of the church. He says that their job is to equip the saints for the work of ministry. That is the work of service. The work of serving one another. The job of all of us in the church is to serve one another. The apostle Paul in Romans 12:4-8 says, "For as we have many members in one body, but all the members do not have the same function, so we, being many, are one body in Christ, and individually members of one another. Having then gifts differing according to the grace that is given to us, let us use them: if prophecy, let us prophesy in proportion to our faith; or ministry, let us use it in our ministering; he who teaches, in teaching; he who exhorts, in exhortation; he who gives, with liberality; he who leads, with diligence; he who shows mercy, with cheerfulness."

The point he is making is that we have been given gifts by the Holy Spirit. The abilities we have were given by the Lord; and it is our responsibility to use those gifts to be a blessing to other members of the church. There are so many ways that we can serve one another in the Lord. Every time somebody bakes a pie or fixes a meal for someone who has just gotten home from the hospital, or takes food to the home of someone who is grieving because a loved one has passed away, he or she is serving in the name of the Lord. When someone visits a brother or sister in the hospital, or runs an errand for someone who is crippled and can't get out, that person is serving a brother or sister. When we reach out to others and do jobs for them, whether it's changing a light bulb, mowing a lawn, or shoveling snow, we are being servants, and that word diakonos would apply to us, not in a formal way, but in a way that we, in the goodness of our heart, reach out and do the job of being a help to others.

The other thing that I wanted to point out is in that sixth chapter of Acts and in other places the job of the deacon is to administer the benevolence of the church. They were taking care of the widows. They were getting food and other support to the widows. That is exactly as it should be.

When we were in Missouri, one of our deacons in the church was on the roof of his house putting on a new roof when he had a heart attack. By the grace of God, he was able to get down off the roof and go to the hospital in time. He was okay. He couldn't finish putting the roof on his house, so the rest of the deacons in the church went to his house and finished putting the roof on for him. It was a great thing, but it was the kind of thing we should be doing all the time. Realizing that, they began to look around and find people who had needs that they could serve. I was in the home of one of our couples who were both in their nineties. I was sitting there visiting with them; and I looked up and noticed that their ceiling was about to fall down. It was in really bad shape. I took note of it and talked to the man who was the chairman of the deacons and told him about it. He said he would go and see them. He went by to see them and visit with them. After he talked with them for a while, he asked them if they would like to have a new ceiling. They knew he was a contractor, so they said they would love one but couldn't afford one. They got a new ceiling anyway because the deacons were looking for ways to serve. That's really the way we all ought to be. We ought to be looking around at our brothers and sisters so we can see things they need. We should be reaching out to them and doing what we can to help them. That's the spirit of service that Jesus teaches us.

There was a young woman in our church who was in training to be a nurse. Her husband was stricken with an incurable disease and was unable to earn a living for his wife and little child. His disability check barely kept them going. When he passed away, they had no income. The church decided to give her monthly support until she finished nursing school. After she got a job as an R.N., she began repaying the church. This is also the kind of thing deacons could administer.

You know He talked about dividing the sheep from the goats; and He said to the sheep on his right, "'Come, you blessed of My Father, inherit the kingdom prepared for you from the foundation of the world: for I was hungry and you gave Me food; I was thirsty and you gave Me drink; I was a stranger and you took Me in; I was naked and you clothed Me; I was sick and you visited Me; I was in prison and you came to Me.' Then the righteous will answer Him, saying, 'Lord, when did we see You hungry and feed You, or thirsty and give You drink? When did we see You a stranger and take You in, or naked and clothe You? Or when did we see You sick, or in prison, and come to You?' And the King will answer and say to them, 'Assuredly, I say to you, since you did it to one of the least of these My brethren, you did it to Me'" (Matthew 25:34-40).

That is how we are to function as members of the Lord's church. We are to always be looking for ways we can be of service to one another in the Lord.

Stephen

"And Stephen, full of faith and power, did great wonders and signs among the people. Then there arose some from what is called the Synagogue of the Freedmen (Cyrenians, Alexandrians, and those from Cilicia and Asia), disputing with Stephen. And they were not able to resist the wisdom and the Spirit by which he spoke. Then they secretly induced men to say, 'We have heard him speak blasphemous words against Moses and God.' And they stirred up the people, the elders, and the scribes; and they came upon him, seized him, and brought him to the council. They also set up false witnesses who said, 'This man does not cease to speak blasphemous words against this holy place and the law; for we have heard him say that this Jesus of Nazareth will destroy this place and change the customs which Moses delivered to us.' And all who sat in the council, looking steadfastly at him, saw his face as the face of an angel." Acts 6:8-15

Now, from Acts 7:51-60, this is the close of Stephen's testimony before the highest council of the Jews,

"'You stiff-necked and uncircumcised in heart and ears! You always resist the Holy Spirit; as your fathers did, so do you. Which of the prophets did your fathers not persecute? And they killed those who foretold the coming of the Just One, of whom you now have become the betrayers and murderers, who have received the law by the direction of angels and have not kept it.'

When they heard these things, they were cut to the heart, and they gnashed at him with their teeth. But he, being full of the Holy Spirit, gazed into heaven and saw the glory of God, and Jesus standing at the right hand of God, and said, 'Look! I see the heavens opened and the Son of Man standing at the right hand of God!'

Then they cried out with a loud voice, stopped their ears, and ran at him with one accord; and they cast him out of the city and stoned him. And the witnesses laid down their clothes at the feet of a young man named Saul. And they stoned Stephen as he was calling on God and saying, 'Lord Jesus, receive my spirit.' Then he knelt and cried out with a loud voice, 'Lord, do not charge them with this sin.' And when he had said this, he fell asleep."

Most people want to be the best they can be. I know I want to be the best husband, the best father, the best neighbor, and the best friend I can be. I want to be the best preacher, and the best teacher, and the best student of the word, and the best follower of Jesus I can be. And when people think of me, if they think of me, I want them to think I was a man who was very serious about following Jesus, a man who truly had a hunger and thirst for righteousness, a man who sought first the kingdom of God and His righteousness.

But sometimes in our desire to follow Jesus, we are distracted by worldly things. So many mundane things that demand our time, our energy, our attention. In spite of everything, I still have to take out the garbage. I still have to mow the lawn or get someone to do it for me. I still have to do the dishes and fold the clothes (sometimes). So, we're distracted by all these different things; and besides that, we sometimes get discouraged when we do give the best we have; and nobody seems to appreciate it.

Some of you work your fingers to the bone, and the boss doesn't even seem to notice. Some of you have sacrificed greatly for your children, and they just seem to take it for granted as if somehow you owed it to them. So, we get discouraged; we need someone to rekindle the flame in us, someone to light our fire, to recharge our batteries, and get us started again on our quest to become all God wants us to be. For me, there is nothing that inspires me more than the story of a life well lived. Of course, the ultimate story of such a life is the story of Jesus. The writer of Hebrews says, "Let us run with endurance the race that is set before us, looking unto Jesus, the author and finisher of our faith, who for the joy that was set before Him endured the cross, despising the shame, and has sat down at the right hand of the throne of God" (Hebrews 12:1-2). He is the ultimate inspiration. I'm reminded of the song that says, "Lest I forget Gethsemane, lest I forget thine agony, lest I forget thy love for me, lead me to Calvary."

The story of Jesus going to the cross for us because He loved us is the most inspirational story ever told. There has never been anything to compare with it; and there never will be. As I heard James Dobson say, "If that doesn't light your fire, your wood must be wet."

But sometimes we need to hear other stories that inspire, stories of imperfect people who lived their lives well. I love the story of Eric Liddle, who was called "the flying Scotsman" because he could run so fast. He was a rugby player in Scotland and was well known in that country. In 1924, he entered the Olympic Games being held in Paris. His race was the 100 meters, but he was disqualified because he refused to run in a qualifying heat that was run on Sunday. Before anything else, Eric Liddle was a Christian. He believed it would not be right for him to compete on the Lord's Day. So, he ran in the 400-meter race instead. It was not his race, but they entered him anyway. All he did was win the race, earn the gold medal, and set a world record.

He enjoyed the acclaim for a short while, then he made his way to China where he served as a missionary alongside his parents. During World War 2 he was captured by the Japanese and placed in an internment camp. The conditions were horrible. They lived in a squatter and were given barely enough food to survive. Eric Liddle died in that camp because he was always giving his food to someone else. The story of Eric Liddle inspires me because, more than anything else, He wanted to walk in the footsteps of Jesus.

In the Bible, other than Jesus, no one is more inspiring to me than Stephen. Stephen lived the way I want to live, and he died the way I want to die. Let me clear that up. I don't want to be stoned to death. But Stephen died without fear, with love for his enemies in his heart, and the name of Jesus on his lips.

Let's take a look at what we know about Stephen. He was one of the first seven deacons who were chosen by the church in Jerusalem to do the job of distributing food and other necessities to the widows in the church. There were thousands of men in the church in Jerusalem at that time. Out of all those men, the church chose seven. Stephen was one of them. He could have refused. He could have said, "I'm too busy. I've got too many things to do. Please get someone else." But he didn't. He accepted the responsibility. I believe it was because he was a man of compassion. The Bible tells us he did great wonders and signs among the people. Surely some of those miracles involved healing the sick. Almost every time you see someone in the New Testament other than Jesus performing a miracle, it is a miracle of healing. I believe Stephen looked around and saw people in need. The apostles had laid their hands on him and given him the power to heal the sick. It must have been a source of joy to him to be able to heal those who were sick. I think he was truly a man of compassion.

There was a man named Giles Tate. He was walking by a vacant lot one day. He saw some children playing there who looked like they were hungry. He stopped to talk with them and discovered they were living in an old, abandoned school bus with their father who was very ill. He took their father to the hospital where they discovered he had tuberculosis. Then Mr. Tate stood in the hall outside his room. They wouldn't let him go in because Tuberculosis is an infectious disease. He stood out there and read the scriptures to him and led him to Christ. He also paid his hospital bill. Giles Tate saw those children and their father with eyes of compassion. He reached out and gave himself and what he had to meet their needs. Like Stephen, he inspires me because he was a man of compassion.

Stephen was also a student of the Word. He was well prepared when he debated with the men from the synagogue of freedmen. They could not overcome his wisdom and his logic and his knowledge of the word of God. He was well prepared. You and I need to be students of the Word as well. The scriptures tell us that we should be able to give a reason for the hope within us whenever we are asked. Let me give you a suggestion. If you have Mormons come to your door trying to sell you their brand of religion, show them Mark sixteen, verses 15 and 16, where it tells us that Jesus said to His apostles, "Go into all the world and preach the gospel to every creature. He who believes and is baptized will be saved; but he who does not believe will be condemned." Then you can tell them that you believe in Jesus and you have been baptized, so you know you have been saved, and you don't need what they are selling. If they persist, you can show them Galatians 1:8, "But even if we, or an angel from heaven, preach any other gospel to you than what we have preached to you, let him be accursed." Their so-called angel who brought them a different gospel, according to this scripture, is accursed.

Here's another suggestion. Inside the front cover of your Bible write a scripture reference. In the margin of that passage write another reference. Then just keep going like that until you have led them to see their need for salvation right through belief, repentance, confession, and baptism. You can end with Acts 22:16 where Ananias says to Saul, "Now why wait, arise and be baptized, and wash away your sins calling on the name of the Lord."

This is a list of Scriptures you can use like that:

Romans 3:23, Romans 6:23, John 3:16, Hebrews 11:6, Acts 17:30, Romans 10:9-10; Acts 2:38, Mark 16:16, Romans 6:3-4, Acts 8:35-38, Acts 22:16

We need to be prepared so we can give a reason for the hope that is within us, so we can lead others to commit to Jesus Christ. Stephen was a bold and courageous leader who used the gifts God had given him to touch other lives for the Lord. He did something else that no one else did. He debated with Jews from the synagogue of freedmen. It didn't bother him that no one else had done it that way. Sometimes a person in the church will have an idea about how to do something that is bold and innovative; and we say, "We've never done it that way."

We need to be bold and courageous. We need to not let anything stop us, other than a clear indication from the Word that it shouldn't be done that way. We need a way of presenting the gospel to this generation that they will respond to. I am not suggesting that we go outside of the parameters laid down for us in the Bible, but anything that is within those parameters, we should use to reach people for Jesus.

Stephen was also a man who obviously spent time with the Lord. The Bible tells us that Moses spent time on the mountain in the presence of the Lord; and when he came down from the mountain, his face glowed. We don't read that Stephen's face glowed, but it does say that his face was like the face of an angel. Perhaps it was the calmness, the serenity, and the pure joy they saw that made it seem like the face of an angel.

When we have been in the presence of Jesus through prayer, the world will be able to see that there is something different about us.

When the council gave Stephen a chance to speak for himself, he used the time to speak to their needs. He showed them that throughout their history, the people of Israel had been rebellious, then he showed them they were no better. Their fathers had killed the prophets; and they had followed in their footsteps and murdered the Just One God had sent to be their Savior.

They could not deny what he said or refute it, so they became furious and rushed at him like a mob. They seized him, dragged him out of the city, and stoned him to death. As he was dying, he showed how much he wanted to be like Jesus. He prayed for his enemies. He said, "Lord, do not charge them with this sin" (Acts 7:60).

I'm reminded of a story Robert Schuler told about a man he called Aaron. He was a young man who was a seminary student in Chicago. At the end of one semester, he was hoping to get a job in some kind of ministry where he could use his ability in serving the Lord, but no job opened up for him like that, so he took a job driving a city transit bus. One day, a group of young thugs got on the bus and passed right by without paying their fare. So, he called out to them and told them they needed to pay. They just laughed at him, ridiculed him, and mocked him. He didn't do anything else. He just let them ride until they got off. This happened several days in a row until finally one day he saw a policeman standing on a corner. He stopped the bus and called the policeman. When the policeman got on the bus, he told him what had been happening. The policeman told the thugs they could either pay or get off the bus. Grumbling, they paid. But then the policeman got off the bus. After they travelled a little farther and turned a couple of corners, the thugs came forward and beat the young man severely. When he woke up, the bus was empty, he had two missing teeth, and both eyes were bruised and swollen. He took the bus back to the terminal and went home. As he lay in the bed he thought, "Why? I asked the Lord for a ministry. Why has He allowed this to happen to me?" Then another thought came. The next day he found the policeman and pressed charges against the young men.

They were all rounded up and brought to court. On the day of their court appearance, they all pleaded guilty. Then Aaron stood up and asked if he could speak. When he was given permission, he said, "Your Honor, I would like for you to add up all the days you are planning to sentence these young men to and let me serve those days for them." The judge said, "You're out of order. You can't do that. It's never been done before." Aaron said, "OH, yes, it has. More than nineteen centuries ago, Jesus went to the cross to pay the penalty for each of us." The judge allowed him to speak for two or three minutes telling the court about Jesus. Then he sentenced the young men to jail, and Aaron went to the jail day after day and talked to them about Jesus. Several of them were converted. He had a ministry. It wasn't the one he had hoped for, but it was an opportunity to show them the Spirit of Jesus by the things he did.

Stephen was a man of God who sought first of all to be the man Jesus wanted him to be. He was a man of compassion. He was a bold and courageous leader. He lived as I want to live; and he died as I want to die. I hope that all of us will be inspired by Stephen.

Discussion Questions
Chapter 6

1. When you think of deacons in the church today, what do you think they are selected to do?

2. If deacons are servants, what are some things they could be doing to serve the church? Should they focus on serving the people or on the church as an organization, such as serving as treasurer or trustee?

3. Do we have people in the church who need our help, as the widows did in the early church? How could we determine if they were truly desperate? How could we keep from enabling lazy, unworthy people?

4. What would you think was Stephen's greatest asset? Boldness? Knowledge of the Scriptures? Intelligence? Courage?

5. Why did the apostles insist on men of integrity for the first deacons?

6. How should we go about choosing deacons today?

Chapter 7

The Samaritan Revival

"Therefore, those who were scattered went everywhere preaching the word. Then Philip went down to the city of Samaria and preached Christ to them. And the multitudes with one accord heeded the things spoken by Philip, hearing and seeing the miracles which he did. For unclean spirits, crying with a loud voice, came out of many who were possessed; and many who were paralyzed and lame were healed. And there was great joy in that city. But there was a certain man called Simon, who previously practiced sorcery in the city and astonished the people of Samaria, claiming that he was someone great, to whom they all gave heed, from the least to the greatest, saying, 'This man is the great power of God.' And they heeded him because he had astonished them with his sorceries for a long time. But when they believed Philip as he preached the things concerning the kingdom of God and the name of Jesus Christ, both men and women were baptized. Then Simon himself also believed; and when he was baptized, he continued with Philip, and was amazed, seeing the miracles and signs which were done.

Now when the apostles who were at Jerusalem heard that Samaria had received the word of God, they sent Peter and John to them, who, when they had come down, prayed for them that they might receive the Holy Spirit. For as yet He had fallen upon none of them. They had only been baptized in the name of the Lord Jesus. Then they laid hands on them, and they received the Holy Spirit.

And when Simon saw that through the laying on of the apostles' hands the Holy Spirit was given, he offered them money, saying, 'Give me this power also, that anyone on whom I lay hands may receive the Holy Spirit.'

But Peter said to him, 'Your money perish with you, because you thought that the gift of God could be purchased with money! You have neither part nor portion in this matter, for your heart is not right in the sight of God. Repent therefore of this your wickedness, and pray God if perhaps the thought of your heart may be forgiven you. For I see that you are poisoned by bitterness and bound by iniquity.'

Then Simon answered and said, 'Pray to the Lord for me, that none of the things which you have spoken may come upon me.'"
Acts 8:4-24

This chapter is called "The Samaritan Revival." Of course, the word revival is not found in the scriptures, but a little research will reveal that this word refers to a time when there is widespread rekindling of interest in spiritual matters. It is, for our purposes, a time when many people respond to the gospel of Jesus Christ and commit their lives to Him. Those lives are transformed to the point that society itself is impacted by what is happening.

By that definition, there have been some revivals that took place in America. The first of them happened after that time our country was very young, from about 1790 until 1810. It was called by some the Second Great Awakening. During that time, a man named Timothy Dwight was the president of Yale. He preached in the chapel at Yale every day. As a result of his preaching and other influences, almost the entire student body turned to Jesus Christ. The impact of what took place at Yale spread throughout the colonies. It was in that context that Alexander Campbell,

Barton W. Stone, Racoon John Smith, and Evangelist Benjamin Franklin in Ohio preached a message that was gladly received by the people. During that time, the churches of the restoration movement made up the fastest-growing movement in the United States. The Millennial Harbinger, which was published by Alexander Campbell and written by him and his young protégé Robert Richardson, became the most popular religious periodical in the United States. Truly, it was a time of revival. Across the frontier, whole churches were turning from their denominational background, realizing that if they returned to the Bible as the only authority for the faith and practices of the church, they could be Christians only. They understood that they didn't need to be members of any denomination. They could just be Christians. By that definition, what was happening in Samaria could be called a revival.

Here is how it happened. After the stoning of Stephen, there arose a terrible season of persecution of Christians. It was led by a young man called Saul of Tarsus. They went from house to house and compelled Christians to deny the name of Christ or be killed or sent to prison. There is no record of any of them ever faltering. So far as we know, they all remained true to Christ, but the persecution caused them to flee from Jerusalem. Wherever they went, they preached the gospel. Only the apostles remained in Jerusalem. The devil tried to destroy the church at its foundation, but it backfired on him. The scattered church became a missionary church. They took the message with them throughout the Roman Empire.

Jews from all over the empire had come to Jerusalem for the Feast of Weeks, called Pentecost. While they were there, the church was born, and many of them became a part of it. So, when the Jewish feast was over, they stayed there. When the persecution began, they decided it was time to go home. Wherever home was, they took the gospel there. Luke says that they went everywhere preaching the gospel. When they got home, they talked to their families about Jesus. They talked to their friends and anyone else who would listen. Pockets of Christianity sprang up all over the Roman Empire.

Philip was among those who left the capital city. He probably remembered that the gospel said, "You shall be witnesses to Me in Jerusalem, and in all Judea and Samaria, and to the end of the earth." (Acts 8:4-24) So, he thought, "Nobody has taken the message to Samaria yet. I'll go there." He took the gospel to Samaria, and because he was one of those on whom the apostles had laid hands, he was able to perform miracles of healing. So many of the Samaritans were converted that they are called multitudes.

It says there was great joy in that city. Let's think about that for a moment. What was it about the message of Philip that made so many of them respond to it? No doubt the miracles of healing he performed gave powerful testimony to the fact that he was a messenger sent by God. The God he represented was merciful and kind because he healed so many people and delivered so many from the demons that controlled them. Beyond that, he could give a powerful personal testimony about what God had done for him.

He could tell them about the many thousands of people who were turning away from Judaism and embracing Christianity. He could tell them about how their lives were transformed so that they actually lived by the principle of loving your neighbor as yourself. They expressed that love by taking care of the widows. In fact, there was no one in the church in Jerusalem who was destitute because they were taking care of each other. He could tell them about the hundreds of people in Jerusalem who had actually seen Jesus alive after He arose from the grave. He could tell them of the many miracles that happened in Jerusalem.

Let me point out something to you. At this point in the Book of Acts, there are only fourteen people who are said to have performed miracles, the twelve apostles and Stephen, and Philip. So only the apostles and those on whom they had laid their hands and imparted to them the spiritual gift were enabled to do what they did. Let me ask you, "What made you decide to follow Jesus?" I dare say that in most cases, there was someone who was a genuine Christian, someone whose faith was real, whose faith brought joy and peace to his or her life, who made you think that this was real. We know that the Bible says, "Faith comes by hearing, and hearing by the word of God" (Romans 10:17). So, the Holy Spirit indeed influenced you through the word, but beyond that, there was some person who made serving Jesus attractive to you. It may have been your parents. It may have been a Sunday School teacher. I remember a teacher I had as a very small boy, Mrs. McGee. It was obvious to us that she loved us and loved teaching us, so we loved her in return. As I look back, I think she had an impact on my life. Of course, my parents had the biggest impact. The point I am making is that most of us encountered someone who was a genuine Christian, who made following Jesus something we wanted to do. We saw a sweetness, a generosity, a kindness, a peace, and a joy in them, and we knew that Christian faith made life worth living.

We read that the people of Samaria received the message with great joy. We might ask, "What was there about it that produced such joy?" I believe they heard for the first time in their lives that the God of heaven loved them dearly. They knew that their first ancestors lived in a paradise with God, but they forfeited that paradise by sinning. They knew that they were also guilty of sin, so they had no right to live in Paradise with God. It was a new revelation to them that God loved them so much that He was willing to allow His Son to die for them. But then, He brought Him back to life again, and hundreds of people saw Him after He arose. This message of God's love that made it possible for them to have the promise of a home in paradise, where they could be with their loved ones and enjoy fellowship with God for eternity, was wonderful news. The gospel is good news for all of us. There was joy in Samaria because of a message of hope and love.

Isn't it interesting that many children, when they have received a spanking, the first thing they want to do is climb up in Momma's or Daddy's lap. They want to be reassured that Momma or Daddy still loves them even though they did something wrong. I believe that deep down in our hearts, we have that same desire. We know we have done wrong. We know we don't deserve a home in heaven, so it is with great joy that we learn that we can be forgiven, and our Father in heaven still loves us, and still wants us to be with Him in heaven.

The story goes on to tell us about a man named Simon. He had practiced sorcery for many years in Samaria and tricked many people there into believing he was a great man of God. When Simon saw real power, He recognized it. He saw something far different from what he was doing. He saw a power that was used to bless people, that was never used to exploit them. There was one person who knew what he was doing was a hoax, a lie. That was Simon, himself. He was convinced that Philip was truly a messenger sent by God, so Simon surrendered his life to Jesus and was baptized. He became a Christian and an avid follower of the ministry of Philip. He was fascinated by what he saw.

When the apostles in Jerusalem heard about what was happening in Samaria, they sent two of their number to give some aid and comfort to the

Christians there and to do what only they could do to strengthen the church in Samaria. Part of their purpose in coming was to impart certain gifts of the Spirit to Christians in Samaria. Philip possessed the gift of healing, but he could not pass it on to others. This passage in Acts shows us that only the apostles could impart spiritual gifts to others through the laying on of their hands.

There were several different gifts that were given this way. Paul discusses this in 1 Corinthians 12:4-11.

"There are diversities of gifts, but the same Spirit. There are differences in ministries, but the same Lord. And there are diversities of activities, but it is the same God who works all in all. But the manifestation of the Spirit is given to each one for the profit of all: for to one is given the word of wisdom through the Spirit, to another the word of knowledge through the same Spirit, to another faith by the same Spirit, to another gifts of healings by the same Spirit, the working of miracles, to another prophecy, to another discerning of spirits, to another different kinds of tongues, the interpretation of tongues. But the same Spirit works all these things, distributing to each one individually as He wills."

Paul told the Romans, "For I long to see you, that I may impart to you some spiritual gift, so that you may be established" (Romans 1:11). He was given the ability to pass those gifts to others just as the other apostles.

Just as an aside. If Peter had been a pope, he would have done the sending of a delegation of apostles to Samaria. Verse 14 says, "Now when the apostles who were at Jerusalem heard that Samaria had received the word of He, they sent Peter and John to them." There was no pope for another three hundred years.

The authority was vested in all twelve of the apostles. I don't know why the apostles stayed in Jerusalem at this time. Perhaps it was so that churches all over the empire would have a central authority located there to whom they could appeal if there was a problem they didn't know how to solve. They did spread out later and take the gospel to other places. The apostle Peter went to areas north of where Paul went in Galatia. Diane and I had the privilege of travelling to India several years ago. We conducted evangelistic meetings in the southern part of the country. The tradition there is that the apostle Thomas brought the gospel there. One section in India is more Christian than any other. It is there they say that he came.

In this passage of Acts, we are told that Peter and John came to Samaria. When they arrived, they laid hands on some of the Christians for the purpose of imparting spiritual gifts. Luke says they received the Holy Spirit. It was His presence in them that brought the spiritual gifts. In the New Testament, we read about three different measures in which the Holy Spirit is given. The first was the baptism of the Holy Spirit, which came on the day of Pentecost only to the apostles. The second came to the household of Cornelius, the first Gentile group to hear the gospel (Acts 10:44-45). They were given the ability to speak in other languages, but not the other powers that were given to the apostles. These were the only two times when the baptism of the Holy Spirit was given. This second baptism of the Holy Spirit was God's way of showing the apostles and the rest of the church that God was accepting Gentiles as well as Jews into His kingdom.

The second measure of the Holy Spirit given at that time was the Spiritual Gifts. This measure of the Spirit's presence was given through the laying on of an apostle's hands. The powers they were given were for the purpose of confirming their testimony about Christ. The apostle Paul teaches in 1 Corinthians 13:11 that these powers were needed when the church was in its infancy, but would be put away when the church was mature. He speaks metaphorically about the church, saying, "When I was a child, I spoke as a child, I understood as a child, I thought as a child; but when I became a man, I put away childish things." When all of those who had received these gifts from the apostles had died, the age of miracles ended.

In Samaria, when Simon, the former sorcerer, saw what happened, he asked to purchase the power of giving spiritual gifts to others. Peter quickly let him know that no one could purchase the gift of God with money and that he should repent and ask God for forgiveness.

The third measure of the Holy Spirit's presence is called "the gift of the Holy Spirit." It is given to everyone when they are baptized into Christ. Another way of expressing this truth is used by the apostle Paul in Galatians 3:27, "For as many of you as were baptized into Christ have put on Christ." The Holy Spirit fills us and gives us comfort and the assurance of salvation. He also gives us strength and the ability to walk faithfully in the footsteps of Jesus.

The miraculous gifts of the Spirit ceased after the New Testament age. Such things as being able to heal the sick, being able to speak in languages we have never studied, being able to translate those languages, and being able to prophesy future events came to an end after the church reached about one hundred years old. When all of the apostles and all those on whom they had laid hands had passed from this life, the miracles ceased. That is not to say that God never works miracles today. He does answer our prayers, but there are no special people who exercise the ability to work miracles. I can lay my hands on someone and pray for healing; and if it is His will, He can work a miracle. But I don't have any greater power than you do; and neither does anyone else. You have the power of prayer just as I do. God still works miracles, but it is not through certain individuals who have been given power.

There was a great revival in Samaria. The Bible tells us that multitudes believed. The city itself was impacted by what was happening. God can still bring revival to our world in the twenty-first century. Please join me in praying that we will be able to see such a time in our lives.

Philip and the Ethiopian

"Now an angel of the Lord spoke to Philip, saying, 'Arise and go toward the south along the road which goes down from Jerusalem to Gaza.' This is a desert. So, he arose and went. And behold, a man of Ethiopia, a eunuch of great authority under Candace the queen of the Ethiopians, who had charge of all her treasury, and had come to Jerusalem to worship, was returning. And sitting in his chariot, he was reading Isaiah the prophet. Then the Spirit said to Philip, 'Go near and overtake this chariot.'

So, Philip ran to him, and heard him reading the prophet Isaiah, and said, 'Do you understand what you are reading?'

And he said, 'How can I, unless someone guides me?' And he asked Philip to come up and sit with him. The place in the Scripture which he read was this:

'He was led as a sheep to the slaughter;
And as a lamb before its shearer is silent,
So He opened not His mouth.
In His humiliation His justice was taken away,
And who will declare His generation?
For His life is taken from the earth.'

So, the eunuch answered Philip and said, 'I ask you, of whom does the prophet say this, of himself or of some other man?' Then Philip opened his mouth, and beginning at this Scripture, preached Jesus to him. Now as they went down the road, they came to some water. And the eunuch said, 'See, here is water. What hinders me from being baptized?'

Then Philip said, 'If you believe with all your heart, you may.'

And he answered and said, 'I believe that Jesus Christ is the Son of God.'

So, he commanded the chariot to stand still. And both Philip and the eunuch went down into the water, and he baptized him. Now when they came up out of the water, the Spirit of the Lord caught Philip away, so that the eunuch saw him no more; and he went on his way rejoicing. But Philip was found at Azotus. And passing through, he preached in all the cities till he came to Caesarea." Acts 8:26-40

After the tremendous impact of the preaching of Jesus in Samaria, it seems strange that the Holy Spirit would pull Philip out of there to send him to a single man. Once again, the wisdom of the Lord is shown in this. The individual was a powerful and influential government official from Ethiopia. He had made the long trip to Jerusalem (about 1500 miles) to worship, most likely for one of the great feast days. If we assume they rested on the Sabbath, it would have taken about ten weeks to make the trip. It certainly indicates he was a devout man; and when we read that Philip heard him (v. 30) reading from the book of Isaiah, it only adds to our impression of his devotion. It also indicates that he must have had a driver and that it was a large vehicle that could accommodate another passenger when he invited Philip to come sit with him.

"Traveling carriages of the first century often had four wheels and were covered, offering protection from the elements and more space for luggage and passengers. Such carriages would allow for more extended periods of travel in greater comfort" (Wikipedia). They traveled about 25 miles per day on average.

The man's question gave Philip the perfect opportunity to present the gospel. There is no other passage from Isaiah that so clearly shows that the Messiah would suffer to provide salvation for the world. The Holy Spirit was in control of the situation. He led the man to that particular passage at that precise time. The preaching of Jesus to him obviously contained instructions concerning how to claim that salvation through faith and obedience, including baptism. He would not have known to ask to be baptized if Philip had not taught him about it. There is another fact revealed in this story. A candidate for baptism was required to acknowledge his faith through confession before he was baptized. When Philip stated that he could be baptized if he believed, he said that he believed that Jesus Christ is the Son of God.

At that point, the man commanded his driver to stop the chariot (v. 38), and both he and Philip went down into the water, and Philip baptized him. The only reason they both went down into the water was that baptism was administered by burying the person in the water and raising him up out of the water. Any other way of baptizing could have been done without it being necessary for both of them to go down into the water.

Discussion Questions
Chapter 7

1. Why do you think the people of Samaria reacted overwhelmingly to the message Philip preached?

2. Do you think Simon, the sorcerer, was truly converted?

3. Peter told Simon to repent and pray to God, if perhaps the thought of your heart may be forgiven you? Was he skeptical of Simon's sincerity? Why else would he include the word perhaps?

4. When the apostles sent Peter and John to Samaria, do you think the whole group decided to send them? Who was in charge?

5. Did anyone ask you if you believed that Jesus is the Christ before you were baptized? How old would a child have to be to answer that question?

Chapter 8

The Conversion of Saul

"Then Saul, still breathing threats and murder against the disciples of the Lord, went to the high priest and asked letters from him to the synagogues of Damascus, so that if he found any who were of the Way, whether men or women, he might bring them bound to Jerusalem. As he journeyed, he came near Damascus, and suddenly a light shone around him from heaven. Then he fell to the ground and heard a voice saying to him, 'Saul, Saul, why are you persecuting Me?' And he said, 'Who are You, Lord?' Then the Lord said, 'I am Jesus, whom you are persecuting. It is hard for you to kick against the goads.' So he, trembling and astonished, said, 'Lord, what do You want me to do?' Then the Lord said to him, 'Arise and go into the city, and you will be told what you must do.' And the men who journeyed with him stood speechless, hearing a voice but seeing no one. Then Saul arose from the ground, and when his eyes were opened, he saw no one. But they led him by the hand and brought him into Damascus. And he was three days without sight, and neither ate nor drank.

Now there was a certain disciple at Damascus named Ananias; and to him the Lord said in a vision, 'Ananias.' And he said, 'Here I am, Lord.' So the Lord said to him, 'Arise and go to the street called Straight, and inquire at the house of Judas for one called Saul of Tarsus, for behold, he is praying. And in a vision he has seen a man named Ananias coming in and putting his hand on him, so that he might receive his sight.' Then Ananias answered, 'Lord, I have heard from many about this man, how much harm he has done to Your saints in Jerusalem. And here he has authority from the chief priests to bind all who call on Your name.' But the Lord said to him, 'Go, for he is a chosen vessel of Mine to bear My name before Gentiles, kings, and the children of Israel. For I will show him how many things he must suffer for My name's sake.'

And Ananias went his way and entered the house; and laying his hands on him he said, 'Brother Saul, the Lord Jesus, who appeared to you on the road as you came, has sent me that you may receive your sight and be filled with the Holy Spirit.' Immediately there fell from his eyes something like scales, and he received his sight at once; and he arose and was baptized. So when he had received food, he was strengthened. Then Saul spent some days with the disciples at Damascus." **Acts 9:1-19**

This story about the conversion of Saul is certainly one of the most dramatic on the pages of the New Testament. It must be very important because it is told three times in the book of Acts. The first one is here in chapter nine. Luke, in the course of his narrative about what was going on in the early church, tells this story. It is told again in chapter twenty-two and again in chapter twenty-six. In those places the apostle Paul is giving his testimony about how he came to know the Lord.

Let's take a closer look at what happened. After the stoning of Stephen there arose a great persecution of the church. That persecution was led by this young man named Saul of Tarsus. He was completely sincere in what he was doing. He believed it to be the will of God. They would go into houses and drag out Christians and seek to make them deny the name of Christ. There is no record of anyone who denied Him.

In order for them to do what they were doing, the Roman authorities had to look the other way. The Jews were not allowed to execute anyone. Apparently, the Romans didn't care that they were doing this, so they looked the other way. The effect of the persecution was exactly opposite of what the persecutors and Satan intended. The devil wanted to stamp out Christianity before it could spread, but those who were scattered went everywhere preaching the gospel. Rather than stamp it out, what he did was spread it.

A great many of those who had come to Jerusalem for the Feast of Weeks, called Pentecost, were from places all over the Roman empire. They had stayed there when they became Christians. They did not want to be separated from their new brothers and sisters in Christ. They didn't want to leave this rich fellowship. When the persecution arose, they decided it was time to go home. When they got there, they began to tell everyone about Jesus. So, little pockets of Christianity began to spring up everywhere. That is to say, churches began to appear in various locations throughout the empire.

It must have been about this time that Saul got word that there was a significant number of Christians in Damascus. So, he went to the High Priest and got a letter from him, that is, a commission, to go to Damascus and seek out the Christians, bind them, and bring them back to Jerusalem for punishment. Now, he couldn't do that without the permission of the Romans. Again, they looked the other way. They simply could not have gone into another country, kidnapped people there, and returned them to Jerusalem for punishment without the tacit approval of the Romans.

That was what Saul intended to do. He was headed to Damascus with a contingent of men, probably armed, to carry out the plan. But God had other plans. As they got close to Damascus, a light shone down on them from heaven which was brighter than the noonday sun. It was focused on Saul, but they all saw it and fell to the ground in fear. They heard a voice speaking to him, but they couldn't understand what they were hearing.

The others did not look into the light. It was literally blinding. Saul looked into the light as the voice spoke, 'Saul, Saul, why are you persecuting me?" Saul responded, "Who are you, Lord?" The Lord said, "I am Jesus, whom you are persecuting. It is hard for you to kick against the goads." Saul was trembling in fear when he asked, "What do you want me to do?" The Lord told him to get up and go into the city where he would be told what to do.

When the light went away, Saul was blind, but he told the men to take him into the city. There, he stayed in the home of a man named Judas on Straight Street. In ancient cities the streets were very narrow and winding. If you go to Damascus today, you can see within the ancient city a straight street. It was on that street that Saul lodged. For three days, he fasted and prayed in anguish of heart. Then the Lord sent a man named Ananias to him to instruct him in the way of Christ. He first touched Saul, and something like scales fell off his eyes; and he could see again. When Ananias had completed the instructions, he said, "And now why are you waiting? Arise and be baptized, and wash away your sins, calling on the name of the Lord." I want you to notice this, Saul believed in Jesus. He had repented too, but his sins had not been washed away. That happened when he was baptized. Did the water wash away his sins? No, of course not. God washed away his sins when he demonstrated his faith by allowing himself to be baptized in the name of Jesus. So, when he had been baptized, they gave him some food. The terrible guilt that led him to fast had been taken away by the mercy of the Lord.

I find there are several very important lessons to be learned from this story. The first is that God's wisdom is far greater than what we can imagine. Who in the world other than God would choose his fiercest opponent to be his greatest advocate? Here was a man who was doing everything in his power to stamp out Christianity; and God chose him to become the great apostle to the Gentiles. The wisdom of His choice can be seen in the fact that there was no one in the first century who did as much to promote Christianity as Paul. Beginning in Antioch of Syria and going on into Cyprus, then Pisidia, and what is now Turkey, then Macedonia, and Greece, and Italy, and all the way over to Spain, all the countries along the northern side of the Mediterranean Sea were evangelized by this man. Almost all of the Roman Empire heard the gospel because of the work of this man. There were millions of people who heard the gospel and became Christians because of the work of Paul.

Then, of course, he also wrote thirteen books of the New Testament, from Romans through Philemon and perhaps Hebrews. In addition, he was the influence behind two other books. Luke was a traveling companion and co-worker with Paul. He was the author of the gospel of Luke and the book of Acts. The gospel of Luke is the gospel that Paul preached. While the apostle was in prison in Caesarea, Luke was able to interview eyewitnesses to the earthly ministry of Jesus. He indicates he did that in the opening verses of his gospel. We are pretty sure the gospel was written during that time. Then he traveled to Rome with Paul when he was sent there for trial. During those years, he wrote the book of Acts, which ends with the apostle still in prison there. That's how Acts ends with Paul still awaiting trial before Caesar. Why else would he stop there other than the fact that he had caught up to the time then present. In all, almost one-half of the New Testament was written by Paul or one of his traveling companions. It is impossible to overestimate the impact of his ministry. The man who had been the greatest enemy of the church was transformed by God into its greatest advocate. The wisdom of God is beyond what we can imagine.

It was not unusual for God to make choices that would have baffled us at the time. He chose a spoiled, arrogant teenage boy named Joseph and taught him humility by allowing his brothers to sell him as a slave. When he was falsely accused and thrown in prison, he learned to trust in God even in the worst of circumstances. When the Lord arranged for him to become the right-hand man to Pharaoh, he was able to save his family from the famine that devastated that whole area for seven years.

He also chose another spoiled, rich young man named Moses, who thought he was something special, to lead His people out of Egypt and mold them into a nation. Stephen tells us that Moses thought the people of Israel would understand that God had chosen him to be their leader to deliver them from their bondage (Acts 7:25). But he had to flee from Egypt and spend forty years in Midian working as a shepherd to learn how to be humble and depend on God. It was only then that God sent him back to Egypt to lead His people to freedom. He became the greatest leader the world had ever known until Jesus came.

God also chose a coward named Gideon when he was hiding in a wine press because he was afraid of the Midianites. He was threshing out a little wheat for his family when God called him. The Lord transformed him into a powerful military leader who was able to deliver his people from their oppressors. God is able in His wisdom to find people and transform them into the leaders He wants them to be.

The second lesson to be learned from this passage of Scripture is that God is powerful. Saul was on his way to Damascus with an armed force. I'm sure he thought he had plenty of power to do what he planned to do, but then he came face-to-face with real power. He must have wondered why this great God did not crush him like a bug. He had been fighting against his God, doing everything he could to oppose the true people of God. He knew he had been spared for some reason, so he cried out, "What would You have me do?"

That power that confronted Saul is still at work in the world today. We can access that power through prayer; and we need to do just that. God could, if He wanted to, transform a leader of Hamas or of Russia into a mighty force for good. God has the power to transform people and make them into the people He wants them to be. We need Him to raise leaders who can impact our society and lead us into a new age of godliness.

Finally, this passage of Scripture shows us the magnificent love of God. It shows us a man who was fighting against God with all his might, and yet God loved him. The Lord reached out to him and transformed him and made him into the great apostle Paul.

There was an old Scottish shepherd who had a lovely daughter who was very precious to him. She loved to go to the fields with him and hear him call out to his sheep with a peculiar, musical call, which the sheep would hear and come rushing to him. When she grew up, she decided to go into the city to find a job. For a while, she wrote him letters regularly. Then the letters came less frequently; and finally, they stopped altogether. Sometime after they stopped, the old shepherd found someone to look after his sheep, and he went to the city to find her. He did not have an address. He did not know how to find her, so he did the only thing he could think of. He walked up and down the streets of that great city, calling out as if calling his sheep. Finally, on one of the back streets of that city, in a run-down part of town, in an upper room of a sleazy apartment building, a young woman heard her father's voice and ran down to him. She threw herself into his arms; and he took her home and won her back to himself and to God. The old shepherd did not care if the people of that city thought he was crazy. He only cared about one thing, bringing his daughter home.

The Blessing of Persecution

"So when he had received food, he was strengthened. Then Saul spent some days with the disciples at Damascus. Immediately he preached Christ in the synagogues, that He is the Son of God. Then all who heard were amazed, and said, 'Is this not he who destroyed those who called on this name in Jerusalem, and has come here for that purpose, so that he might bring them bound to the chief priests?' But Saul increased all the more in strength, and confounded the Jews who dwelt in Damascus, proving that this Jesus is the Christ.

Now after many days had passed, the Jews plotted to kill him. But their plot became known to Saul. And they watched the gates day and night, to kill him. Then the disciples took him by night and let him down through the wall in a large basket.

And when Saul had come to Jerusalem, he tried to join the disciples; but they were all afraid of him, and did not believe that he was a disciple. But Barnabas took him and brought him to the apostles. And he declared to them how he had seen the Lord on the road, and that He had spoken to him, and how he had preached boldly at Damascus in the name of Jesus. So he was with them at Jerusalem, coming in and going out. And he spoke boldly in the name of the Lord Jesus and disputed against the Hellenists, but they attempted to kill him. When the brethren found out, they brought him down to Caesarea and sent him out to Tarsus.

and were edified. And walking in the fear of the Lord and in the comfort of the Holy Spirit, they were multiplied." Acts 9:19-31

Saul of Tarsus was a troublemaker. Everywhere he went, he stirred up trouble. In Jerusalem he participated in the stoning of Stephen, and led the charge in the continued persecution of Christians, dragging them out of their homes and attempting to force them to deny Christ. Some were killed, and others were thrown into prison.

He was traveling to Damascus to continue harassing the church when he met Jesus face to face. It was the turning point in his life. He began immediately preaching Jesus as the Christ. Trouble still seemed to follow him everywhere. In Damascus, the enemies of Christ planned to murder him, but the disciples helped him escape by lowering him through the wall in a basket. It seems very strange to us, but there were actually homes built up against the city walls; and a few of them had windows in the walls. Apparently, one of those homes was occupied by a Christian family and was used to provide a means of escape for Saul.

After that he went to Jerusalem. He tried to join the disciples there, but they didn't trust that he had actually been converted. Barnabas decided to take a chance with him and discovered he was sincere; so, he took him to meet the apostles. Once he was accepted, he began preaching in Jerusalem, and once again they plotted to kill him. When the brethren found out about the plot, they sent him home to Tarsus. When he was gone, things settled down in Jerusalem, Judea, Galilee, and Samaria, and the church prospered.

Jesus had said, "Blessed are you when they revile and persecute you, and say all kinds of evil against you falsely for My sake. Rejoice and be exceedingly glad, for great is your reward in heaven, for so they persecuted the prophets who were before you" (Matthew 5:11-12). This passage from Acts reveals why we should rejoice when persecution arises.

The persecution of Saul tested and strengthened his faith. It began almost immediately in Damascus, and forced him to consider if he had done the right thing in becoming a follower of Jesus. Of course, he passed the test with flying colors. Some people falter when faced with difficulties. Others become stronger. Saul was one of those. The more he was persecuted, the more he was determined to keep the faith.

The opposition also required him to know why he believed; so, he became very skilled in presenting the proof from Old Testament scriptures concerning God's plan to use a suffering Savior to provide salvation to those who believe in Him. Those who tried debating him soon discovered they could not succeed. Their only choice was to accept the truth he proclaimed or get rid of him. They decided on the latter, but they succeeded only in getting him to move on to another place to preach.

Saul's experience with persecution has been repeated over and over again to the point that it is generally accepted that persecution is the lifeblood of Christianity. Wherever it happens, the church grows stronger, and individual Christians experience joy in the Lord. They find that Jesus really is with them always.

Richard Wurmbrand tells of his experiences of persecution at the hands of Communists in his book, Tortured for Christ. He was arrested in Romania and imprisoned for preaching the gospel. In prison, he continued preaching and was subjected to severe torture. When telling his story to the American Congress, he removed his shirt to show them nine deep scars caused by the torture. He said that Jesus was never more real to him than when he was being tortured. He tells of a time when they caused him to stand facing a white wall lighted with powerful lights. It was so bright that it was painful to look at it, but if he closed his eyes for a second, they would strike his back with a painful blow. They caused him to stand there for more than 24 hours like that, but it did not stop him from preaching. Even in solitary confinement he talked to the prison guards about Jesus. It seems to be the universal reaction of those who suffer persecution for Christ. He is very real to them and gives them comfort.

Persecution produced humility in Saul, who came to be known as the apostle Paul, the one God commissioned to be the apostle to the Gentiles. When he learned of the plot to kill him in Damascus, he hid from his enemies who were watching the gates so they could not apprehend him trying to escape. His departure was in a rather humbling way as he was lowered in a basket from a window in the city wall. He later wrote to the Romans and admonished them concerning humility, "For I say, through the grace given to me, to everyone who is among you, not to think of himself more highly than he ought to think, but to think soberly, as God has dealt to each one a measure of faith" (Romans 12:3).

It seems to me that Paul's boldness in proclaiming the gospel even in places he knew were likely to persecute him was related to his experience as a persecutor. He wanted to make amends for his former conduct. He was humbled and ashamed by what he had done. He knew his salvation was a gift he could not earn, but he felt a debt he wanted to pay. He said, "I am a debtor both to Greeks and to barbarians, both to wise and to unwise. So, as much as is in me, I am ready to preach the gospel to you who are in Rome also. For I am not ashamed of the gospel of Christ, for it is the power of God to salvation for everyone who believes, for the Jew first and also for the Greek (Romans 1:14-16).

We need to pray for the courage to tell others about Jesus as he did. It may mean we will be ostracized, but it is a very small price to pay, and it puts us in the company of the prophets and others who suffered for the Lord. We also must be humble as he was. We would have no hope of heaven except for His grace. When we approach others, it must always be with the realization that we are no better than they are. We mustn't come across as ones who have a "holier than thou" attitude. We cannot expect to be received every time. If we are rebuffed, we must remember to keep on loving them and seeking to show Christ's love to them.

We must also be patient. We may be misunderstood even by brethren. Just keep on praying, and learn to rejoice in any discomfort we may experience in our service to Him and others. And never stop. It is too important to let a little discouragement keep us from witnessing for Him.

In addition, note his wisdom. When the brethren in Jerusalem sent him back to his home in Tarsus, he went without complaining. It would be nice to know about his activities in his hometown. I am sure he was not idle. There were probably many converts in Tarsus, but it did not contribute to Luke's narrative to include that story. I'm sure also that Saul would have loved to have been in the thick of the struggle in Jerusalem, but he saw a vision of the Lord telling him to, "Make haste and get out of Jerusalem quickly, for they will not receive your testimony concerning Me." He says in Galatians 1:21-23 that he preached in Syria and Cilicia. It was several years later when Barnabas invited him to join him in the work in Antioch. We don't always know the best path to follow, so it behooves us to pray for direction and accept the fact that He has given us the wisdom He promised when we make a decision. "If any of you lacks wisdom, let him ask of God, who gives to all liberally and without reproach, and it will be given to him" (James 1:5).

In every age, dedicated Christians are persecuted. Sometimes it is by other Christians who consider them fanatics. They are misunderstood and not appreciated. We must learn to be thankful for our hardships because they help to mold us into the servants God wants us to be. Rejoice because great is your reward in heaven.

Discussion Questions
Chapter 8

1. When were Saul's sins washed away? Is that true for all of us?

2. Do you think Ananias was courageous when he went to meet Saul? Would you have been afraid to go to him?

3. Do you think people are still being persecuted for following Jesus? Would the authorities have the evidence to convict you of being a Christian if you were arrested?

4. Why do you think Paul always stirred up the enemies of Christ when he came to town?

5. How would we be treated if we went into the stronghold of other religions to preach Jesus?

Chapter 9

The Spiritual Leader

"Then the churches throughout all Judea, Galilee, and Samaria had peace and were edified. And walking in the fear of the Lord and in the comfort of the Holy Spirit, they were multiplied.

Now it came to pass, as Peter went through all parts of the country, that he also came down to the saints who dwelt in Lydda. There he found a certain man named Aeneas, who had been bedridden for eight years and was paralyzed. And Peter said to him, 'Aeneas, Jesus the Christ heals you. Arise and make your bed.' Then he arose immediately. So all who dwelt at Lydda and Sharon saw him and turned to the Lord.

At Joppa there was a certain disciple named Tabitha, who is translated Dorcas. This woman was full of good works and charitable deeds which she did. But it happened in those days that she became sick and died. When they had washed her, they laid her in an upper room. And since Lydda was near Joppa, and the disciples had heard that Peter was there, they sent two men to him, imploring him not to delay in coming to them. Then Peter arose and went with them. When he had come, they brought him to the upper room. And all the widows stood by him weeping, showing the tunics and garments which Dorcas had made while she was with them. But Peter put them all out, and knelt and prayed. And turning to the body he said, 'Tabitha, arise.' And she opened her eyes, and when she saw Peter, she sat up. Then he gave her his hand and lifted her; and when he had called the saints and widows, he presented her alive. And it became known throughout all Joppa, and many believed in the Lord. So it was that he stayed many days in Joppa with Simon, a tanner." **Acts 9:31-43**

Peter was and always will be one of the greatest leaders in the history of the church, but he was not a pope. The doctrine of the supremacy of the bishop of Rome was not well established in the Catholic church until around 440 A.D. In the New Testament, all of the elders were called bishops. It was simply another title given to the local leaders of the church. The word translated bishops (Philippians 1:1) means, simply, overseers. Acts 20:12 tells us that Paul summoned the elders of the church in Ephesus. When they came, he addressed them, and admonished them to "take heed to yourselves and to all the flock, among which the Holy Spirit has made you overseers" (V. 28). The word translated overseers is the same word which is translated bishops in Philippians 1:1. From this passage we learn that elders and bishops (or overseers) are both terms used to refer to the leaders of the local church. They were the shepherds and overseers of local congregations. It was later that one elder was elevated over his fellow elders in a particular location and referred to as a bishop.

This passage, Acts 9:31-43, shows us a great example of what a leader in the church should be. After Saul had been sent to Tarsus, things settled down to a time of peace for the churches in Judea, Galilee, and Samaria. Peter wisely seized the opportunity to tour the churches in all parts of the country. Apparently, the peaceful times allowed Christians to travel freely without fear of arrest. It was a perfect time for Peter to make this tour to bring encouragement to the churches.

When he came to Lydda, he found a man named Aeneas who was paralyzed and had been bedridden for eight years. Peter spoke to him saying, "Aeneas, Jesus the Christ heals you. Arise and make your bed." The man arose immediately, and when word of his healing was known, people all over the region turned to the Lord.

Prosperous times often are challenging for Christians. They can settle into a routine that makes them comfortable to the point of lulling them to sleep with no great feeling of needing the Lord's direction in their daily lives. It's almost as if they are thinking, "It's O.K. Lord, I've got this." In times of persecution, Christians are painfully aware of their need for God, but it may not be so evident to them in times of peace.

Jesus may have been thinking of such times when He told the parable of the Sower and the Seed. He said, "Now he who received seed among the thorns is he who hears the word, and the cares of this world and the deceitfulness of riches choke the word, and he becomes unfruitful" (Matthew 13:22). We get caught up in the mundane things of everyday life, our jobs, our children, their education, the need to buy groceries. We don't feel the need for His help in these things. We have to plan meals, make a grocery list, mow the lawn, make the mortgage payment, get the oil changed and the tires rotated, do the laundry, wash the dishes, run the vacuum cleaner, go to our son's ballgame, the list is unending. We have to remind ourselves to take time for Bible reading and prayer. It becomes almost imperative to schedule a time for daily devotions. It is so easy to push our worship time to the "back burner." We should make it part of our daily prayers to ask the Lord to slow us down enough to enjoy His presence.

While Peter was in Lydda, the Christians in Joppa were mourning the loss of a beloved sister in Christ. Dorcas was a loving lady who spent her time doing good for others. She devoted herself to sewing and making garments for them. In their grief, they sought the comfort a great man of God could bring to them, so they sent to Lydda to see if Peter could come.

They did not seem to think of him raising her back to life. It is probably true that they had heard about the healing of Aeneas; and maybe some of them hoped Tabitha (or Dorcas) would be raised. Others just wanted to hear comforting words from Peter. When he arrived, the widows were showing the garments she had made for them. To their surprise, Peter put them out of the room. He knelt and prayed and then turned to the body and said, "Tabitha, arise." The Lord used his servant Peter to bring this dear lady back to life. Peter took her hand, helped her to her feet, called the widows and other Christians back, and presented her alive. The story of this miracle soon circulated all through the area, and many more people were led to believe in Jesus.

We can learn from these two examples that it is important for those of us who are leaders in the church to show compassion to those who are grieving as well as those who are sick. Elders, deacons, and others who serve as leaders in the church should always visit the sick to offer encouragement. In the case of infectious diseases, we don't want to be spreaders of the disease, but we can serve by phoning them and praying for them, and running errands for them. If our compassion is real, we will find ways to be helpful to them.

These examples from the ministry of Peter demonstrate two facets of the work of church leaders: ministering to the needs of Christians and leading the lost to salvation in Jesus. In my own ministry, I found a tension between these two responsibilities. When I wanted to be reaching out to the lost, I needed to be preparing for teaching the word to His people; and when I was studying, I needed to be visiting the lost. I found I needed to pray for wisdom in dividing my time. What I really needed was two of me.

Cornelius

"There was a certain man in Caesarea called Cornelius, a centurion of what was called the Italian Regiment, a devout man and one who feared God with all his household, who gave alms generously to the people, and prayed to God always" (Acts 10:1-2).

Sometimes we meet people who are not Christians who hold themselves to high moral standards. They can be more worthy of imitation than many who are members of the church. They may be kind and compassionate. They may volunteer for projects in the community that are designed for the benefit of the people. They give generously to charity. They are helpful to their neighbors. In short, they are good people, but they are lost without Jesus. I was once talking with a man about his spiritual condition. I asked him, "What would you say if the Lord asked you, 'Why should I welcome you into heaven?'" He responded that he hadn't done anything to deserve hell.

He needed to know that the Bible says, "All have sinned and fall short of the glory of God" (Romans 3:23). He also needed to know, "The wages of sin is death, but the gift of God is eternal life in Christ Jesus our Lord" (Romans 6:23). The story of Cornelius is a story of a good man who was lost without the salvation Jesus provides. I wonder how many people there are who feel confident that they haven't done anything to deserve hell.

Cornelius was a man who would seem to be in great shape, one who could have thought he was doing everything God would expect a man to do, but he still needed what only Jesus can offer. No one can say in truth that he or she has never lied or cheated anyone, spoken a profane word or lusted after some beautiful woman or handsome man. There are numerous commands that we fail to obey. How about, "But I say to you, love your enemies, bless those who curse you, do good to those who hate you, and pray for those who spitefully use you and persecute you?" (Matthew 5:44) The standards of personal conduct set by Jesus in the sermon on the mount are higher than any of us will ever achieve. It doesn't take an evil life to be judged and found wanting. All of us need Jesus. Without Him we are lost. Only He can forgive us and pardon us and transform us into people prepared to live in the presence of our holy God.

Let's take a look at Cornelius. He was a centurion in the Roman army in what was called the Italian Regiment. Centurions were what we call non-commissioned officers. They typically had 80 troops in their command. The Romans called the troops Legionnaires because they were a part of a Roman legion. Their regiment was called an Italian regiment because all the soldiers were from Italy. In many Roman regiments the soldiers were from conquered nations. They would typically impress young men from the conquered nation into their army to provide a police force for their own nation. They were unable to do that in Israel because the young men would not cooperate. Consequently, they had to have an occupying force in Israel.

There are four other centurions mentioned in the New Testament. The first centurion was from Capernaum. He asked Jesus to heal a beloved servant who was paralyzed and near death. When Jesus said he would come and heal him, the centurion responded by saying, "I did not think myself worthy to come to You, but say a word and my servant will be healed." The story is found in Matthew 8:5-13 and in Luke 7:1-10. The centurion also indicated that he understood authority. He said he could tell a servant to do something, and that servant would do it. He was indicating that Jesus had the authority to command the forces of nature, and they would obey. With our knowledge of sickness and disease, we would say that he could destroy bacteria or reverse the effects of disease by just saying the word.

Jesus marveled at the faith of that centurion.

He had sent some elders of the Jews to ask Jesus to heal his servant. Those elders told the Lord that the centurion was worthy because he loved their nation and had built them a synagogue. Archaeologists discovered in Capernaum the ruins of an ancient synagogue. Although it was not the one that was in Capernaum when Jesus preached there, it was built on the foundation of the synagogue from the first century, which was probably the one the centurion built.

Another centurion was in charge of the lictors who carried out the crucifixion of Jesus. Lictors were name given to a group of four soldiers who crucified those who were condemned. When he saw what happened when Jesus died, the darkness that covered the land, the earthquakes, and the cry from the lips of Jesus just before he died (Mark 15:37), the centurion said, "Truly this was the son of God." (Matthew 27:54) When victims were crucified, they died by suffocation. While hanging on the cross, fluid built up in their lungs until it prevented them from breathing. In the last moments before death, they would not be able to cry out with a loud voice as Jesus did. It was not suffocation that took the life of Jesus. The fact that both blood and water flowed from the wound when the spear was thrust into his side (John 19:34) indicates that the pericardium was filled with blood. That would only happen if his heart had burst. When the centurion heard the loud cry, he knew that Jesus did not die as other men die.

One other centurion is mentioned in the New Testament, his name was Julius of the Augustan regiment. He was given the job of accompanying Paul and the other prisoners on the trip to Rome, where he was to stand trial. The story is told in Acts 27. The ship that was carrying them encountered a violent storm on the Mediterranean Sea. After about 14 days they realized they were approaching an island which turned out to be Malta. The pilot of the ship tried to sail into a bay with a beach. They hoped to get close to the beach before running aground, but they got stuck in the sand some distance from the beach. The soldiers intended to kill all the prisoners because if they escaped, the soldiers would have been executed. The centurion, to save Paul, allowed all the prisoners to swim ashore. It turned out that they all were saved, and none of the prisoners escaped.

The general impression we get from these stories of centurions in the New Testament is that they were honorable men. At least two of them were godly men.

We want to take a closer look at Cornelius. Acts 10:2 tells us, "He was a devout man and one who feared God with all his household, who gave alms generously to the people, and prayed to God always."

It is evident from these stories from the New Testament that it was possible for a soldier to be a godly man. We know that there are some occupations that are not compatible with Christianity. I don't believe you could sell pornography or dope and be a faithful Christian. I don't think I could be a good soldier because I'm not sure I could kill an enemy even if he was trying to kill me, but I believe that others could do that with a clear conscience. Sergeant York was a highly decorated soldier from World War One; and he was also a devout Christian. A job allows one to make a living. Our relationship with Jesus allows us to make a life.

The scripture says that Cornelius feared God with all his household. His religion was not an outward show. It was inward, a religion of the mind, the heart, the conscience, and the will. Jesus told us that the greatest commandment is to love God with all the heart, the soul, and the mind. (Matthew 22:37) Our faith comes from hearing the word of God, considering the evidence, and deciding to believe. It is an exercise of the mind. Our commitment to Christ is an act of our will. Loving God with the whole heart is the response of our emotions as well as an act of our will. Loving Him with our whole soul involves actively living for Him. The word soul actually means life. Our soul is our life.

When the scripture says that Cornelius feared God with all his household, it shows his influence on those around him. His household would have included his servants as well as his family. In Acts 10:27, it says that when Peter came into the house to speak to Cornelius and his family, he found that many had gathered there. In verse 7, it says he sent two of his household servants and a devout soldier to summon Peter. One wonders how many of the soldiers in his command had followed his example in worshipping the Lord.

A man may fool the whole world, but his family will know. If he is sincere and is wise, gentle, loving, and kind as well as firm, they will gladly follow his lead. Cornelius had the respect of his servants and his soldiers as well as his family.

The scripture also says he "gave alms generously to the people." His religion and love for people expressed themselves in a practical way. Jesus was talking about men like him in Matthew 25 when he said, "Come, you blessed of my Father, inherit the Kingdom prepared for you from the foundation of the world: for I was hungry and you gave Me food; I was thirsty and you gave Me drink; I was a stranger and you took Me in; I was naked and you clothed Me; I was sick and you visited Me; I was in prison and you came to me." When they asked when they ever saw Him in any of those conditions, He replied, "Since you did it to one of the least of these My brethren, you did it to Me."

Cornelius showed his compassion by acts of kindness to his neighbors. If we want to gain the approval of our Father in heaven, we will do the same thing. James 1:27 says, "Pure and undefiled religion before God and the Father is this: to visit orphans and widows in their trouble, and to keep oneself unspotted from the world."

Finally, the scripture says that Cornelius prayed to God always. If we are to be true and faithful children of God, we must be people of prayer. The Jewish people had regular hours of prayer each day, every morning and every evening at the time of the daily burnt offering. At that time the devout were expected to pray. When Jesus was about to begin his ministry, He spent 40 days in the wilderness fasting and praying to His father in heaven. If Jesus needed to pray, we certainly need to also.

I wonder what percentage of Christians in America set aside a time for prayer each day. I have found through experience that God answers prayer often. We just need to recognize it and thank him for it.

We have seen that Cornelius had a great many things for which he was to be commended. We could say that, according to the understanding he had at the time, he was a sincere man of God. Yet, he was lost because he didn't know Jesus. No one comes to the Father except through Jesus. Our Savior said, "I am the way, the truth, and the life. No one comes to the Father except through Me" (John 14:6). It does not matter how morally upright a man may be, he will not make it to heaven unless he has obeyed the gospel of Jesus Christ.

Discussion Questions
Chapter 9

1. Why did a man as good as Cornelius need to hear the gospel?

2. Does God still speak to people in dreams? Have you ever had a strong feeling that God was directing you to do something?

3. When you were baptized, did you feel like you were cleansed?

4. Why do people look to their preacher for comfort in times of mourning?

5. What do you suppose was Tabitha's first thought when she awoke and saw Peter there? Did she know she had just been raised from the dead?

Chapter 10

Peter Challenged

"Now the apostles and brethren who were in Judea heard that the Gentiles had also received the word of God. And when Peter came up to Jerusalem, those of the circumcision contended with him, saying, 'You went in to uncircumcised men and ate with them!' But Peter explained it to them in order from the beginning." **Acts 11:1-4**

When Peter returned to Jerusalem after preaching to the household of Cornelius, the leaders of the church there challenged him concerning what he had done. But instead of challenging his decision to preach the word to the Gentiles, they criticized him for going into their home and eating with them. They could hardly complain about the change in the lives of those who heard the gospel, so they questioned his violation of their traditions. No law from the Old Testament prevents such action. It is often the case that traditions are held on to more tenaciously than the gospel.

Peter's defense is masterful. It provides an example for us should we ever face a similar situation. He began by relating the story of his vision on the housetop. It showed how God had prepared his mind and heart to receive the truth that God was accepting Gentiles into His Kingdom. He explained to them how God showed him that there are no people who are unacceptable to him because of their race, their nationality, their economic situation, or whether they're male or female. He went on to tell them how the messengers who came from Cornelius had arrived simultaneously with the end of his vision. He also told them that the Holy Spirit had commanded him to go with them without doubting. His third point was that he witnessed the Holy Spirit falling on them in the midst of his presentation of the gospel. He noted that it was just as it happened to them in the beginning, that is, on the day of Pentecost when the Spirit came on the apostles with power. We know it was the baptism of the Holy Spirit that the Father had promised to them. Since he described it in that way, we must conclude that the household of Cornelius also received the baptism of the Holy Spirit. These are the only two cases in the New Testament that can be shown to be baptism. Not many years later, the apostle Paul wrote in Ephesians 4:5 that there is "one Lord, one faith, one baptism." Everyone knows that the church was baptizing new converts in water at that time, so it is still the baptism that the church should practice today. Paul also wrote that we are "buried with Him by baptism." That is the one baptism Paul was talking about. Peter concluded his defense by stating that he had concluded that the Gentiles were accepted on the same basis as they were: by faith in Jesus Christ. It is worth noting that the propriety of accepting Gentiles and baptizing them into Christ was never questioned again in the New Testament church.

There are some important lessons we can learn from this incident. First, we must be careful that we do not allow our traditions to become more important than the plain truth of the Scriptures. The Jewish attitude toward Gentiles did not come from the scriptures but from the tradition of the Pharisees. Their superior, holier-than-thou, attitude resulted in a mutual hatred between Jews and Gentiles. Paul said to the Jews, "The name of God is blasphemed among the Gentiles because of you" (Romans 2:24).

In the Christian churches and churches of Christ, we have our traditions, which are not set in stone, even though we sometimes seem to think they are. For example, we meet on Sunday mornings for worship.

Chances are, in New Testament times, they met on Saturday night. The story in Acts 20 tells of Paul preaching until midnight. At that time a young man named Eutychus fell out of a third-story window and apparently broke his neck. Paul went down and embraced him and restored his life. He then went back and preached until morning. Then they observed the Lord's supper. The first day of the week began for them at sundown on the seventh day, so what we know as Saturday night was the first day of the week for them. If we decide to meet for worship on Saturday night, we will be sharply rebuked by some.

When I traveled to Australia many years ago, I found that they did not have Welch's grape juice. The juice they used was from local grapes. It looked strange to us because it was red instead of purple. If I had brought some of that back with me and used it for the Lord's Supper, I'm sure I would have been questioned about it. I believe every church of Christ I have ever worshipped with followed the same formula for observing the Lord's Supper. They have a prayer before serving the unleavened bread. Then they pray again before serving the "cup." If I were to suggest that they have one prayer and then serve both the bread and the cup, I might be accused of doing it wrong.

Diane and I also travelled to India to conduct evangelistic services in primitive villages there. You would be amazed to see how they observed the Lord's supper. They only used one cup, but it was very sanitary because no one ever touched the cup with his or her lips. They tilted their heads back, held the cup above their mouths, and poured a small amount into their mouths. I never saw anyone spill any of the juice. If I had tried to do it that way, I would have had it all over my shirt. But I certainly did not tell them they were doing it wrong.

People giving testimonies is still rare in our churches. If I were to ask someone to stand and give his or her testimony, people would perhaps think I had gone overboard in many of our churches. There is nothing in the scriptures to suggest there is anything wrong with such a practice, yet we shy away from it because it is done in denominational churches.

There are several things about how this controversy was handled in the church in Jerusalem that are good examples for us if we have a dispute over anything in the church. First, everything was completely open and honest. People often oppose something simply because they do not like change. They want everything to stay the way it has always been, but they don't think their resistance to change will be a good enough reason for others to join them, so they pretend that the change would not be permitted by the scriptures.

When I was in Riverview, Alabama, I decided to use our church bus in a way it had never been used before. Our Vacation Bible School was set to begin on Monday night. Early that day, I drove the bus on a route I had laid out earlier. Every time I saw children out playing, I stopped and asked them if they would like to come to our Vacation Bible School. If they said, "Yes," I went to their door and asked if they would be allowed to ride our bus to our VBS. If the Momma agreed, I stopped there that evening to pick them up. When we got to the church building that night, there were fifty children there already. That was the amount they were expecting. We brought fifty more. We called the bookstore in Montgomery, and the owner opened up at nine o'clock that night so we could get the additional materials we needed for the extra children. We had to divide several of the classes and recruit more teachers. None of that would have happened if I had suggested we try it. Someone would have said, "We have never done it that way."

"Those of the circumcision" in Jerusalem were not devious, they objected because Peter's actions were contrary to their tradition. They did not whisper or plot behind his back. They brought their objection out into the open. They believed that God was not pleased with what Peter did; and they felt it was important to settle this matter lest it get out of hand. So, they went directly to the leaders and lodged their complaint. The leaders apparently understood that God had led Peter to do what he did, so they organized the meeting in a way that would settle the matter once and for all.

Once they had stated their objection, Peter was allowed to explain in detail what had happened. He told them of his vision and that three men had come to him saying that Cornelius had been visited by an Angel who told him to send for Peter. They were expecting Peter to tell them what they should do. He also told them that the spirit had instructed him to go with them without doubting. Then he told them that he took six brethren with him to witness what happened; he also told them how the Holy Spirit had fallen upon them just as he fell on the apostles in the beginning. He even mentioned the baptism of the Holy Spirit, saying that He fell upon them as He had upon the apostles on Pentecost. When they heard the full story, they dropped their objections and glorified God because He was also granting a place to the Gentiles.

Parties on both sides of this controversy acted in good faith and accepted God's will in this matter. If we follow their example of openness and honesty, and if we are willing to accept what we learn to be His will, we will be able to settle disputes without anger or bitterness. We need to follow their example as well as the plain teaching of the New Testament.

One other note. Sometimes we argue over things that aren't worth the trouble. If a matter is of no consequence other than avoiding the possibility of offending someone, then we should do nothing that would cause a brother to stumble.

Peter's Escape

"Now about that time Herod the king stretched out his hand to harass some from the church. Then he killed James the brother of John with the sword. And because he saw that it pleased the Jews, he proceeded further to seize Peter also. Now it was during the Days of Unleavened Bread. So when he had arrested him, he put him in prison, and delivered him to four squads of soldiers to keep him, intending to bring him before the people after the Passover.

Peter was therefore kept in prison, but constant prayer was offered to God for him by the church. And when Herod was about to bring him out, that night Peter was sleeping, bound with two chains between two soldiers; and the guards before the door were keeping the prison. Now behold, an angel of the Lord stood by him, and a light shone in the prison; and he struck Peter on the side and raised him, saying, 'Arise quickly!' And his chains fell off his hands. Then the angel said to him, 'Gird yourself and tie on your sandals'; and so he did. And he said to him, 'Put on your garment and follow me.' So he went out and followed him, and did not know that what was done by the angel was real, but thought he was seeing a vision. When they were past the first and the second guard posts, they came to the iron gate that leads to the city, which opened to them of its own accord; and they went out and went down one street, and immediately the angel departed from him.

And when Peter had come to himself, he said, 'Now I know for certain that the Lord has sent His angel, and has delivered me from the hand of Herod and from all the expectation of the Jewish people.'

So, when he had considered this, he came to the house of Mary, the mother of John whose surname was Mark, where many were gathered together praying. And as Peter knocked at the door of the gate, a girl named Rhoda came to answer. When she recognized Peter's voice, because of her gladness she did not open the gate, but ran in and announced that Peter stood before the gate. But they said to her, 'You are beside yourself!' Yet she kept insisting that it was so. So they said, 'It is his angel.'

Now Peter continued knocking; and when they opened the door and saw him, they were astonished. But motioning to them with his hand to keep silent, he declared to them how the Lord had brought him out of the prison. And he said, 'Go, tell these things to James and to the brethren.' And he departed and went to another place." Acts 12:1-17

This is the first time the government has gotten involved in persecuting the church. The family of Herod was a bloody family. Herod, called "The Great," was the one who killed all the little boys two years old and under trying to destroy the One born in Bethlehem to be King of the Jews. The uncle of the one mentioned here executed John the Baptist. Now this one kills James, the brother of John, and plans to murder Peter as well.

Jesus chose twelve men to be His disciples and later His apostles, but only three of them comprised the inner circle of His friends: Peter, James, and John. They were given special privileges. Only those three beheld Him in His glorious form when He was transfigured before them (Matthew 17:1-8). They were also the only ones who were in the room when He brought the daughter of Jairus back to life (Mark 5:37-43). They were the only ones He permitted to go farther into the Garden of Gethsemane with Him on the night He was arrested (Matthew 26:36-46).

. We know much less about James than the other two. His work was cut short by the evil king. We can surmise that his ministry in Jerusalem must have been noteworthy because he was the first one Herod arrested, even before Peter. The fact that his death pleased the Jews adds to the idea that his ministry was significant, but Luke doesn't give us any information about it. We know that he was the second prominent leader who became a martyr. We don't know how many might have been killed during the first persecution which was directed by Saul of Tarsus.

The extreme cruelty of Herod is clearly seen in his decision to execute all the soldiers who had been charged with guarding Peter. Verse nineteen says that he examined the guards and commanded that they should be put to death. If he questioned all of the soldiers, every one of them could say truthfully that he had been faithful in the execution of his duties. They had no way of knowing that an angel had set him free. He had disappeared without a trace. The only explanation was that his escape was miraculous. Herod knew that, yet he preferred to murder the guards instead of admitting it. The word translated squads in verse four means sets of four. There were four sets of four. He executed sixteen men.

Shortly after his murderous act, Herod moved to Caesarea. God did not allow him to live long after that. He sent an angel to administer the punishment. He struck Herod with worms so that he died. Luke says it was because he welcomed the adoration of the people of Caesarea who proclaimed him a god, but it was surely also a judgment for his evil ways.

Luke then noted that the word of God grew and multiplied. Persecution of Christians always produces growth of the church. A wonderful example from my lifetime occurred late in the twentieth century. Bulgaria was one of the most repressive of the communist countries of Eastern Europe. The church was driven underground. Communism in Bulgaria was finally ended in that country in August 1990. On Easter Sunday, 1991, news reports indicated that one million Christians gathered in downtown Sophia, the capital city, and greeted one another with the words, "He is risen." The population of Sophia at that time was less than 1.2 million. The church had flourished underground during those years of persecution. It always does. The courage and peace in the lives of Christians lead others to want what they have.

I believe it was Richard Wurmbrand who told the story of a preacher in Russia who was confronted by a young Russian army officer. The officer pointed to a picture, an artist's portrait of his idea of what Christ looked like. He said, "It's a lie. Admit it." The preacher calmly said he believed it to be true. The officer drew his pistol, pointed it at the preacher, and once again demanded that he admit it was a lie. The preacher knew that if this man killed him, he would probably not be charged with a crime, but he calmly reaffirmed his faith in Christ. The young officer put his pistol down and grabbed the preacher in a bear hug. "Thank God," he said, "I hoped it was true, but I wanted someone willing to die for Him to tell me about Him." Would you have had the opportunity to tell him about Jesus? We won't know for sure until it happens to us. However, I take comfort in the knowledge that Jesus said, "He who is faithful in what is least is faithful also in much" (Luke 16:10). I have been faithful in the little things; I trust He will make me strong if I must face the big things.

During the time of Peter's captivity, the church was praying for him. I wonder what their prayers were like. McGarvey suggests that they may not have been praying for his release. That was not likely to happen, so they may have been praying that he would be strong and peaceful as he faced death. They were surprised when he showed up at Mary's house. He probably went there because he knew there would be a group gathered there to pray for him. It's interesting to see that once he had shown them he was free, he left without telling them where he was going. If any of the authorities came looking for him, they could tell the truth. They didn't know where he was going. There were many thousands of Christians in Jerusalem at that time. If they had wanted to do so, they could have stormed the prison to set Peter free. Instead, they prayed.

We can always be certain that God knows the best way to answer our prayers. The fact that the Christians were surprised when Peter came to them does not show a lack of faith. They were not surprised that He answered their prayers, but they were surprised by the way He answered them. His ideas are always better than ours. We can always trust His judgment. He will always do what is best, even though we may not think so at the time. It is much easier to look back and say, "God knew what He was doing." Peter knew that God would take care of him. If he enabled him to escape, that would be good; but if he allowed him to die, that would be even better. Peter was sound asleep when the angel came. It shows he wasn't worried.

Sometimes the best thing we can do is flee. If it takes standing up for your faith to please God in a situation, by all means, do it. If you die for it, you will be welcomed home by the Lord. If you can escape without compromising, do that. God will be pleased in that also. Praying with faith means believing God will answer in His time and the way He knows is best.

Discussion Questions
Chapter 10

1. Do you think Peter's explanation satisfied those who challenged him?

2. Do you think Herod thought the soldiers had conspired to release Peter? If not, why did he have them executed?

3. How important are the protections we enjoy in a society that doesn't give anyone the right to order our execution without a trial?

4. Can you think of any places in the world today where Christians are persecuted and sometimes murdered because of their faith? Should we pray for them daily?

Chapter 11

The First Missionaries

"Now those who were scattered after the persecution that arose over Stephen traveled as far as Phoenicia, Cyprus, and Antioch, preaching the word to no one but the Jews only. But some of them were men from Cyprus and Cyrene, who, when they had come to Antioch, spoke to the Hellenists, preaching the Lord Jesus. And the hand of the Lord was with them, and a great number believed and turned to the Lord.

Then news of these things came to the ears of the church in Jerusalem, and they sent out Barnabas to go as far as Antioch. When he came and had seen the grace of God, he was glad, and encouraged them all that with purpose of heart they should continue with the Lord. For he was a good man, full of the Holy Spirit and of faith. And a great many people were added to the Lord.

Then Barnabas departed for Tarsus to seek Saul. And when he had found him, he brought him to Antioch. So it was that for a whole year they assembled with the church and taught a great many people. And the disciples were first called Christians in Antioch." **Acts 11:19-26 (NKJV)**

"Now in the church that was at Antioch there were certain prophets and teachers: Barnabas, Simeon who was called Niger, Lucius of Cyrene, Manaen who had been brought up with Herod the tetrarch, and Saul. As they ministered to the Lord and fasted, the Holy Spirit said, 'Now separate to Me Barnabas and Saul for the work to which I have called them.' Then, having fasted and prayed, and laid hands on them, they sent them away." **Acts 13:1-3 (NKJV)**

The church at Antioch in Syria was the second great church in New Testament times. It was great because it had great leaders. When Barnabas arrived, he found that the church was prospering, for they were determined to reach out beyond the synagogue to lead people to Christ. He encouraged them and joined in the work. At some point, he was led by the Holy Spirit to seek Saul to encourage him to come work with him in Antioch. Saul agreed, and they worked together there for a whole year with great success.

Luke tells us the disciples were first called Christians there. Most commentators believe the pagans gave them that name as a derision. However, the word in the Greek that is translated called, is chrematizo. It means to be called, to be warned, or to be admonished by God. This word is found seven times in the New Testament. Once it is translated as "admonished by God" (KJV) or "divinely instructed" (NKJV). Twice it is translated "called." Four times it is translated "warned by God." In every case, the originator of the communication is God. This fits with the prophecy of Isaiah about a new name to be given to God's people.

> "For Zion's sake I will not hold My peace,
> And for Jerusalem's sake I will not rest,
> Until her righteousness goes forth as brightness,
> And her salvation is a lamp that burns.
> The Gentiles shall see your righteousness,
> And all kings your glory.
> You shall be called by a new name,
> Which the mouth of the Lord will name." **Isaiah 62:1-2**

Note that there were two conditions that had to be met before the new name was given. First, righteousness would shine forth from Jerusalem. That would be the proclaiming of the gospel through which people are endowed with righteousness through Jesus. Second, Gentiles see that righteousness. Antioch was the first church to actively seek to lead Gentiles to Christ. When these two criteria were met, "the mouth of the Lord" gave them a new name.

Now, Luke tells us that this church went a step further as God directed them. Barnabas and Saul were chosen by God and sent out by the church to take the gospel to the Gentile world. The Holy Spirit directed them to separate these two men for the work to which He had called them (Acts 13:2). The leaders obeyed that command by fasting, praying, and laying on of hands. It was apparently a formal ceremony through which they were "ordained" as missionaries. I believe it is an important part of this process to fast and pray. However, I don't think most churches observe this part of the "ordination" of missionaries, elders, deacons, or evangelists. We need to be serious about setting men aside for these tasks. Fasting and prayer before the laying on of hands demonstrates how seriously we take this responsibility.

Why do we ordain men for these jobs? To ordain means to set apart. They are set apart from the world, even from other Christians, so they can dedicate themselves fully to those tasks. We who ordain them should be just as serious about supporting them in every way. When we send out missionaries, we do it because there are millions who are lost in sin; and we have the solution to their problem. The church has a commission to fulfill. Until the whole world hears the message, our obligation has not been satisfied.

Unless we have people who are willing to devote themselves entirely to the task of taking the gospel to the lost world, it will not be done. This task is too important for us to give it less than all we have, all of our minds and hearts. There is no other name under heaven through which they can be saved. We must do everything we can with God's help to get the message out to the world. The magnitude of the task requires absolute dedication.

This is a task worthy of a lifetime of devotion or many lifetimes. In the 1940's J. Russel Morse set out for Asia to take the gospel to nomadic tribes in China and Tibet. Now the fourth generation of the Morse family continues the work in Thailand and Myanmar. They are only one of many such families who have been serving for multiple generations.

The need for more families with noble courage and devotion will never cease until Jesus comes again. Jesus is calling. Who will answer the call?

Fearless

"So, being sent out by the Holy Spirit, they went down to Seleucia, and from there they sailed to Cyprus. And when they arrived in Salamis, they preached the word of God in the synagogues of the Jews. They also had John as their assistant.

Now when they had gone through the island to Paphos, they found a certain sorcerer, a false prophet, a Jew whose name was Bar-Jesus, who was with the proconsul, Sergius Paulus, an intelligent man. This man called for Barnabas and Saul and sought to hear the word of God. But Elymas the sorcerer (for so his name is translated) withstood them, seeking to turn the proconsul away from the faith. Then Saul, who also is called Paul, filled with the Holy Spirit, looked intently at him and said, 'O full of all deceit and all fraud, you son of the devil, you enemy of all righteousness, will you not cease perverting the straight ways of the Lord? And now, indeed, the hand of the Lord is upon you, and you shall be blind, not seeing the sun for a time.'

And immediately a dark mist fell on him, and he went around seeking someone to lead him by the hand. Then the proconsul believed, when he saw what had been done, being astonished at the teaching of the Lord." Acts 13:4-12 (NKJV)

Can you imagine the excitement when Barnabas and Saul started to "go into all the world" with the gospel? If we were the first to send out missionaries into the world, there would be a big celebration as we sent them off. Maybe we would have a marching band. Television cameras would be rolling. The church in Antioch sent them off with fasting and prayer and laying on of hands. It was a thoughtful and prayerful beginning to a great adventure. As for Barnabas and Saul, there could have been some apprehension. They didn't know how the Gentile world would receive their message. In addition, there was always a fear of failure when we human beings attempted something new. It was several years later when Paul expressed his apprehension about going to Corinth, "And I, brethren, when I came to you, did not come with excellence of speech or of wisdom, declaring to you the testimony of God. For I determined not to know anything among you except Jesus Christ and Him crucified. I was with you in weakness, in fear, and in much trembling" (1 Corinthians 2:1-3). They were prepared to face every obstacle, depending on the Lord to be with them always. They were going in obedience to His command; and they had faith in His promise. They proceeded despite any fear with courage and boldness.

The seaport called Seleucia was about sixteen miles away. They may have walked the whole distance in a day, but more likely they took two days. They boarded a ship in Seleucia, which took them to Cyprus. Since Barnabas was leading the endeavor at this time, they went first to the place where he lived. I'm sure he was anxious to share the gospel message with his country. The trip by sea was about a hundred miles. That could have taken as many as four days. We don't know what day of the week it was when they arrived. They planned to begin with the synagogues. So, they waited until the Sabbath to speak at their meetings. The city of Salamis was their starting point. The Jewish people had the background they could use to lead into the story of Christ. They knew that the Jewish people could be a "field white unto harvest." They knew they could be a source of many dedicated followers of Christ. They also knew that it would not be unusual for some of the Jews to oppose them, but they did not let that stop them. They cared too much for the souls of those who would believe to allow the opposition to deter them.

I believe it is high time for us to realize that people will not make it to heaven just because they go to church. Denominationalism is a device of the devil. He uses it to turn people away from the truth. Our spiritual forefathers in the Restoration Movement recognized this and tried to unite all who call themselves Christians by turning them back to looking to the Bible as the only authority for the doctrine and practices of the church. When people cling to their traditions rather than the plain teachings of the Bible, they forfeit the heavenly home they are seeking. We need to get back to calling people to forsake their denominational names and practices. We need to urge all to get back to the Bible.

We are not told of their success or lack of it until they reached Paphos at the opposite end of the island, about one hundred miles from Salamis.

The Roman proconsul was a man named Sergius Paulus. Proconsuls were appointed by the Romans to govern provinces. This man was the governor of Cyprus. He called for the two missionaries; and they came in and preached the word of God to him.

There was in his court a sorcerer named Bar-Jesus or Elymas. He had been successful in persuading the people of Cyprus that he was a great man of God. When Saul and Barnabas began to proclaim the gospel, this man spoke against them, trying to turn the proconsul away from the faith. Saul, filled with the Holy Spirit, rebuked the man, saying, "O full of all deceit and all fraud, you son of the devil, you enemy of all righteousness, will you not cease perverting the straight ways of the Lord? And now, indeed, the hand of the Lord is upon you, and you shall be blind, not seeing the sun for a time" (Acts 13:10-11).

The man was stricken with temporary blindness so that he reached out seeking someone to guide him. When Sergius Paulus saw what happened, he believed. Luke informs us at this time that Saul was also called Paul, and he called the group of missionaries, "Paul and his party" (verses 9, 13). Some think he began to be called by that name because of the name of the proconsul, but I believe it is because that was the Greek equivalent of Saul. From this time forward, he was the leader of the group. There is no indication that Barnabas objected.

From the Cyprian port city of Paphos, they sailed to the port of Perga in Pamphylia. There is no mention of work being done there. They proceeded to Antioch in Pisidia, a distance of about one hundred miles through mountainous terrain. On the Sabbath, they spoke in the synagogue. There were many devout proselytes among the listeners that day; and they begged Paul and Barnabas to return the next Sabbath to tell them more. There were also many Jews who heard the message gladly.

On the next Sabbath, they discovered that those who were anxious to hear more had spread the word, so almost the whole city came to listen. When the unbelieving Jews saw the crowd, they were filled with envy; and they contradicted the word and blasphemed. "Then Paul and Barnabas grew bold and said, 'The word of God needed to be spoken to you first; but since you reject it, and judge yourselves unworthy of everlasting life, behold, we turn to the Gentiles'" (Acts 13:46).

Paul and Barnabas continued to preach in Antioch with great success until the Jews who opposed them stirred up the "devout and prominent women and chief men of the city." The result was the beginning of persecution of the missionaries, which resulted in their expulsion from the region. They shook off the dust of their feet against the oppressors and moved on to Iconium, but the disciples they made were filled with joy and with the Holy Spirit.

Iconium was about 80 miles to the southeast. The trip took them across a vast plain. Iconium was the chief city in that area and a fertile field for the preaching of the gospel. Luke tells us that a great multitude of both Jews and Greeks believed.

The book of Acts doesn't say much about the opposition of pagans at this point, but we would do well to consider the powerful appeal of their worship to carnal mankind. Greek and Roman idol worship included heavy drinking and debauchery. They engaged in gross orgies as a part of their "worship." The closest thing we have in Western society is sex trafficking which is far more common than we realize. It can be seen in the Playboy philosophy and the practices of Jeffrey Epstein and his friends. The horrible debauchery of these people is sickening to anyone who values decency.

It was no small task for an individual to turn away from idolatry to embrace the holiness of the Christian lifestyle. Yet many had already seen the beauty of the Law of Moses with its pure and undefiled way of living.

These were the devout Greeks who were involved with the Jews. They were marginally attached to the synagogues and were immediately attracted to the faith preached by Paul and Barnabas.

These missionaries were offering something far better than the sensual lifestyle of the pagans; they were preaching a religion of noble self-denial, which gives life real meaning and purpose. Real joy is to be found in serving others. There is an inner contentment that comes from knowing you are doing something noble and good rather than just looking out for yourself. Real peace of mind comes from knowing this kind of living pleases God and that heaven is its reward. Knowing your sins are forgiven and that your Father in heaven loves you and is watching over you allows you to be content no matter the outward circumstances.

We must never forget that we have something to offer that is far better than anything the world has to offer. In their sober, thoughtful moments, they know that their lives have no meaning and purpose larger than self. We must, by our acts of kindness and love, show them that our faith is real and that it affects the way we treat others.

The confidence and poise of Paul and Barnabas in the presence of a powerful man showed that they were in the service of One who was far more powerful. In Romans 1:16, the apostle Paul stated that he was not ashamed of the gospel of Christ because it is the power of God that brings salvation to the sinner. It is the power that can change a drunkard into a steady, dependable husband and father. It is the power that can change a criminal into a gentleman and a responsible member of society.

We must not be fearful before the powerful and intellectual leaders of this world. When we come to the end of our lives, we can face death with confidence and serenity because we know the One who gave us life and can give us life eternal. A young girl in the Soviet Union was belittled by a teacher because of her Christian faith. The teacher said, "Our glorious cosmonauts did not see God when they were in space." The girl, in the quiet confidence of one who knows the Lord, responded, "Were they pure in heart? Jesus said the pure in heart will see God."

False prophets are abundant in our land. Many of them are very popular. They have large followings and often have great wealth. We need to expose them and prove they are wrong so the people they have deceived can have an opportunity to learn the truth and be saved. God wants us to be bold, courageous teachers of the truth. We have no reason to be fearful. He has promised to be with us always. We can count on it.

Discussion Questions
Chapter 11

1. How can we use modern technology to get the Word out to the whole world?

2. What percentage of the money collected by our churches should be used for worldwide mission work?

3. What percentage of our income should we as individuals and families give to the work of sending out the message?

4. The preaching of Paul and Barnabas stirred up powerful opposition, but they didn't let that stop them. What keeps us from witnessing to others about our faith?

5. What do you think about athletes who give God the glory when they are interviewed after a game?

Chapter 12

Disposed to Eternal Life

"So when the Jews went out of the synagogue, the Gentiles begged that these words might be preached to them the next Sabbath. Now when the congregation had broken up, many of the Jews and devout proselytes followed Paul and Barnabas, who, speaking to them, persuaded them to continue in the grace of God.

On the next Sabbath almost the whole city came together to hear the word of God. But when the Jews saw the multitudes, they were filled with envy; and contradicting and blaspheming, they opposed the things spoken by Paul. Then Paul and Barnabas grew bold and said, 'The word of God needed to be spoken to you first; but since you reject it, and judge yourselves unworthy of everlasting life, behold, we turn to the Gentiles. For so the Lord has commanded us:

"I have set you as a light to the Gentiles,
That you should be for salvation to the ends of the earth."

Now when the Gentiles heard this, they were glad and glorified the word of the Lord. And as many as had been appointed to eternal life believed.

And the word of the Lord was being spread throughout the entire region. But the Jews stirred up the devout and prominent women and the chief men of the city, raised persecution against Paul and Barnabas, and expelled them from their region. But they shook off the dust from their feet against them, and came to Iconium. And the disciples were filled with joy and with the Holy Spirit." **Acts 13:42-52**

Vernon Newland and his family were placed in an internment camp by the Japanese during World War II. They were serving as missionaries in the Philippines at the time. The Japanese rounded up all foreign nationals and incarcerated them in such camps. When they were processing the missionaries, they asked each of the missionaries if they were Protestant or Catholic. Apparently, they had only those two choices on their forms. When they asked Mr. Newland what he was, he responded that he was neither. He had been teaching the Filipino people that you didn't have to be labeled by such names; you could be just a Christian. By accepting only the Bible as your guide to truth and practice, you could be a Christian only. He could not say he was a protestant without contradicting what he was teaching. The Japanese officer was getting very annoyed with him. Very likely, his life was in danger, but he would not change his answer. A protestant missionary who was present defused the situation by telling the officer Mr. Newland was Protestant. Vernon Newland would not budge from his stance that he was neither Protestant nor Catholic because words are important.

The passage we are considering today contains an idea that is difficult to translate accurately. In the New King James Version of verse 48, the word is translated appointed. It says, "As many as had been appointed to eternal life believed." When you put it that way, it seems to say that God had appointed some to eternal life while others were not appointed. Actually, the word means disposed. It means "those who were disposed by their personalities and upbringing to listen to and seriously consider ideas different from what they had always believed were convinced." They believed because they were willing to believe when the truth was presented to them. The others did not believe because their minds had been made up; and they did not want to be confused by the truth.

Mr. Newland refused to be identified as a Protestant because that label is identified with the teachings of Calvin, such as "unconditional election," which eliminates the element of free will. The people he was teaching would have no confidence in him or his words if he said he was Protestant. He risked his life over the meaning of a word.

If we understand the meaning of this word appointed from verse 48, then verse 46 makes sense. By their disposition to reject the truth of the gospel, they judged themselves unworthy of everlasting life. Their disposition toward unbelief rendered them unworthy of the gift of God.

Let's look at the attitude of the majority of the Jews. At first, they were cautiously tolerant of a different interpretation of the idea of the Messiah. They were accustomed to thinking the prophecies would be fulfilled by an earthly king who would overthrow the Romans and re-establish the kingdom of Israel with all the power and glory of David and Solomon. The idea of a spiritual Savior was novel to them, but they did not immediately reject it. The idea that this salvation was being freely offered to Gentiles as well as Jews was repugnant to them, so their opposition grew with the popularity of the message among the Gentiles. They were proud of the fact that they were God's chosen people, and the idea that He loved the Gentiles just as much as He loved them just didn't go down well. In their attempts to refute the message and contradict the truth, they blasphemed. It must mean that their determined opposition to the gospel led them to speak blasphemous words against it.

By rejecting the truth, they judged themselves unworthy of everlasting life. Their prejudices doomed them to separation from the God who loved the Gentiles as much as He loved them.

The attitude of many of the Jews and devout proselytes was quite different. They were very interested in one who came to offer them salvation and a home with God forever, so they followed Paul and Barnabas after the service ended. They also spread the word all over Antioch so that the next Sabbath day, almost the whole city came to listen to the apostles.

When the opposition of the Jews intensified, Paul and Barnabas declared their intention to turn to the Gentiles. The Gentiles were delighted. Luke says they were glad and glorified the word of the Lord. Then those who were disposed to accept the truth believed. They had never been welcomed as equals by the Jews, so it was wonderful to them to learn of God's love for them. They were glad to be obedient to the faith. Although Luke does not tell of their baptism, they certainly obeyed God's will in this way because throughout the book of Acts, baptism always follows belief and confession.

The sincerity of their faith was illustrated by the fact that they spread the message so enthusiastically that the whole city came together to hear Paul and Barnabas.

The reaction of people everywhere is the same as it was in Antioch. They either receive the word with gladness or they oppose it because they don't want to make the changes in their lifestyle that are required. It behooves all of us to think clearly and soberly about the claims of Jesus. If we truly believe He is the Son of God who died to save us, our only acceptable reaction is total surrender to His will.

Dedication in the Ordinary Man

"Now it happened in Iconium that they went together to the synagogue of the Jews, and so spoke that a great multitude both of the Jews and of the Greeks believed. But the unbelieving Jews stirred up the Gentiles and poisoned their minds against the brethren. Therefore, they stayed there a long time, speaking boldly in the Lord, who was bearing witness to the word of His grace, granting signs and wonders to be done by their hands.

But the multitude of the city was divided: part sided with the Jews, and part with the apostles. And when a violent attempt was made by both the Gentiles and Jews, with their rulers, to abuse and stone them, they became aware of it and fled to Lystra and Derbe, cities of Lycaonia, and to the surrounding region. And they were preaching the gospel there." Acts 14:1-7

There is a canal in Indianapolis. It was there more than 70 years ago when an ordinary man was driving along beside it with his family on a winter day. Then they saw something in that canal that scared them. Two little boys were floundering around in the water, obviously unable to swim. Then that ordinary man did an extraordinary thing. He slammed on the brakes, and as soon as the car rolled to a stop, he was out of it and stripping down to his long-handle underwear. Then he was in the water, swimming to rescue those two little boys. As he set each of them up on the bank, a lady came rushing out of a nearby house with blankets to wrap them all up against the cold.

There was no story in the newspaper, no medal of bravery for that ordinary man. I wouldn't even know that story except my mother never got tired of telling it. That ordinary man was my hero. He was my Dad.

His name was Theodore H. White. No, not the journalist and political writer. They shared the same name, but they had little else in common except that each was 71 years old when he died. Not many people knew my Dad. The people who worked with him through the years, the members of our church, a few neighbors, the people who came to him to have their lawn mowers repaired, and assorted relatives, that is about it.

He never wrote a book, never patented an invention, never built a bridge or a skyscraper, never "made a mark" in his world. But he did other extraordinary things. He loved my mother unconditionally. When she was going through a difficult menopause, he was always patient. He never raised his voice to her. In fact, I never heard them argue. Not once. He always kissed her three times before he left for work each day. Their love never cooled in more than 50 years.

He did make a mark on me and on my brothers and my sister. He set an example that has blessed us all through the years. You can ask my wife if I know how to be a good husband. I have been what my father taught me to be. You can ask anyone who knows me if I am serious about my desire to serve the Lord. It was always evident to everyone who knew my parents that their faith was something to be lived every day.

I grew up in a little house on Raymond Street in Indianapolis. We moved there in 1945. It had two bedrooms, a kitchen, a dining room, and a living room. Oh, it also had a path to the outhouse at the back of the lot. My father put in the indoor plumbing. He managed to find a way to use two closets that were back-to-back to build in a bathroom. When he installed a sink in the kitchen, he built cabinets around it and upper cabinets above it. He installed a water heater and a floor furnace.

At one time, there were seven of us living in that little house: my parents, my two brothers, my sister and I, and my grandfather. You may wonder where in the world we all slept. I'll tell you. Mom and Dad had their own bedroom. The other bedroom provided a place for two of us on bunk beds. Another bed was in a nook in the dining room. In the living room was a couch that could be made into a bed. My oldest brother and my grandfather slept there.

Do you get the idea we were poor, only in material things? That home was filled with love. The love of parents and the love of God. It was also filled with generosity and hospitality, and the rich fellowship of missionaries and evangelists and assorted other men and women of God who visited our church. We always wanted them to come to our house for a meal; and every one of them blessed our lives.

My parents were ordinary people only in the eyes of the world. In the eyes of our Father in heaven, they were extraordinary because they were His children; and they blessed the lives of His other children whenever they met.

A great deal of my understanding of what a father should be comes from my observations of the earthly father God gave me. We don't get to choose our parents. My Father in heaven blessed me beyond measure by the father and mother he gave me.

I tell this story to illustrate that humble dedication to the Savior and to godly living are within the reach of every man and woman and young person. The passage we are studying (Acts 14:1-7) gives us an example of what it takes to be faithful to God, faithfulness for the common man.

Most people at one time or another dream about becoming great. Great success, great accomplishments, great recognition, great wealth, these are the aspirations of most of us. Do you want to be the best Mom or Dad you can be? Do you want to be the best friend or neighbor you can be? Do you want to be the best Christian you can be? Paul and Barnabas, in this passage, give us a great example.

They show us the value of perseverance. When they had to leave Antioch, they moved on to Iconium and began preaching there. When the opposition arose in Iconium, they just kept preaching until it became necessary to leave to save their lives, but that didn't stop them. When they arrived in Lystra and Derbe, they started spreading the gospel there also. They did not let anything stop them. They kept fulfilling their mission with courage and persistence.

You and I can follow their example. Whatever you are doing in church, leading, shepherding, preaching, or teaching, you can hang in there even when no one seems to appreciate you. God takes notice; and the Scriptures admonish and encourage us.

"Come to Me, all you who labor and are heavy laden, and I will give you rest. Take My yoke upon you and learn from Me, for I am gentle and lowly in heart, and you will find rest for your souls" (Matthew 11:28,29). The metaphor of the yoke gives us the picture of Jesus joining with us to pull the load. He will always be with us to lighten our load.

"Therefore, my beloved brethren, be steadfast, immovable, always abounding in the work of the Lord, knowing that your labor is not in vain in the Lord" (1 Corinthians 15;58). The apostle Paul admonishes us to persevere with the assurance that our labor will be rewarded.

One of my favorites, "And let us not grow weary while doing good, for in due season we shall reap if we do not lose heart" (Galatians 6:9). Just keep on, don't let anything stop you. Jesus sees you; and He will reward you in due season.

Paul and Barnabas were a great example of preparation. The first verse of this passage says that they "so spoke that a great multitude both of the Jews and of the Greeks believed." They spoke with great conviction. It was obvious to their audience that these men were absolutely convinced that their message was true. They put all they had into their presentation of the gospel. Not everyone has the talent to be a great speaker, but we all can prepare well. Every moment we spend in the study will be rewarded with greater knowledge and greater ability to present the gospel compellingly. A church member once told me, "I've never known anyone who prepared as you do." That's sad. I would hope that everyone would throw themselves so completely into preparation to speak that it would be obvious to everyone. To give it less than our best is inexcusable. When we repent, Jesus will forgive, but we should make it our goal to be so thoroughly prepared that it is evident to everyone.

They spoke with great power to persuade that included unassailable arguments and undeniable logic. I doubt that they would have been able to do that without many hours of study and additional hours of contemplation of the truth. Perhaps the baptism of the Holy Spirit would have enabled them to do all they did without the hours of study that are necessary for us. I can imagine Paul and Barnabas in deep conversation as they walked for hours from one location to another to spread the word. Their arguments could be refined, and their confidence in the power of the Gospel to convict and convince people to change their lives enhanced during those sessions of discussion of the gospel.

Preparation is the key to being persuasive when we talk to others about Christ. If we spend adequate time in study and in prayer, we can also be persuasive as we present the gospel message. We cannot expect to be powerful and persuasive without thorough preparation.

Paul and Barnabas also spoke with great courage. After a short while, it must have been obvious to them that they should expect violent opposition from both Jews and the government. To keep on preaching would result in persecution, imprisonment, and possibly death. But they also knew that Jesus would never leave or forsake them. That knowledge will give us the courage and conviction we need to persevere and look forward to a crown of righteousness which the Lord will give us when we complete our tasks on earth.

Although we are not likely to have to face violent opposition to our ministries, it still takes courage to speak up for Jesus, but if we do, He will notice and reward us. So, speak up in school, at work, and with friends and family. Let the stories of great courage make you more like Paul and Barnabas; and inspire you to do great things for Jesus and His kingdom.

The Apostles at Lystra

"And in Lystra a certain man without strength in his feet was sitting, a cripple from his mother's womb, who had never walked. This man heard Paul speaking. Paul, observing him intently and seeing that he had faith to be healed, said with a loud voice, 'Stand up straight on your feet!' And he leaped and walked. Now when the people saw what Paul had done, they raised their voices, saying in the Lycaonian language, 'The gods have come down to us in the likeness of men!' And Barnabas they called Zeus, and Paul, Hermes, because he was the chief speaker. Then the priest of Zeus, whose temple was in front of their city, brought oxen and garlands to the gates, intending to sacrifice with the multitudes.

But when the apostles Barnabas and Paul heard this, they tore their clothes and ran in among the multitude, crying out and saying, 'Men, why are you doing these things? We also are men with the same nature as you, and preach to you that you should turn from these useless things to the living God, who made the heaven, the earth, the sea, and all things that are in them, who in bygone generations allowed all nations to walk in their own ways. Nevertheless, He did not leave Himself without witness, in that He did good, gave us rain from heaven and fruitful seasons, filling our hearts with food and gladness.' And with these sayings they could scarcely restrain the multitudes from sacrificing to them. Then Jews from Antioch and Iconium came there; and having persuaded the multitudes, they stoned Paul and dragged him out of the city, supposing him to be dead. However, when the disciples gathered around him, he rose and went into the city. And the next day he departed with Barnabas to Derbe." Acts 14:8-20

When the apostles arrived in Lystra, they encountered a situation that was different from what they were used to. There was no synagogue in Lystra. The gathering place was at the city gates. The men of the city would gather there and discuss the current topic of interest. Paul and Barnabas joined the crowd there and began to preach about Jesus. As they were presenting the gospel, Paul noticed a crippled man who was paying close attention. He perceived that the man had the faith to be healed, so he said to him in a loud voice, "Stand up straight on your feet" (Acts 14:10). The man suddenly jumped to his feet and began to walk. When the people saw what had been done, they began to cry out that the gods had come down to them in the form of men. They thought Barnabas was Zeus and Paul was Hermes. Zeus was the chief of the Greek gods who ruled the other gods from Mt. Olympus. Hermes was his son and spokesman. Then the priest of Zeus brought oxen and garlands to the gate, intending to sacrifice to the apostles. Paul and Barnabas tore their clothes in horror and ran into the crowd, crying out, "Why are you doing these things? We also are men with the same nature as you, and preach to you that you should turn from these useless things to the living God." (Acts 14:14-15). With these protests, they were just barely able to restrain them from offering the sacrifices.

Luke did not tell us what impact these things had in Lystra, because the Jews from Antioch and Iconium came and persuaded the people of Lystra to stone Paul. They probably said something like, "We expelled them from Antioch and Iconium. We were prepared to stone them, but they ran like thieves. They disgrace our nation and perform their wonders through the power of evil spirits. Let us seize their leader, and we can stone him together. So they stoned Paul. When they thought he was dead, they dragged him out of the city and left him there."

There was no mention of any disciples they made there until this point. As they gathered around him, he raised up and went with them into the city. Timothy is not mentioned here, but he was from this area. He was probably a young teenager at this time. Since his mother and grandmother are mentioned in 2 Timothy 1:5 as having been a good influence on him because of their genuine faith, the three of them likely became disciples at this time. There is one other thing that has been connected with this incident by commentators. Paul said to the Corinthians in 2 Corinthians 12:2 that he knew a man who had been caught up into heaven fourteen years earlier. He did not know if he actually went there or if it was a vision. Most people think he was talking about himself, but did not want it to seem like he was boasting of his experiences too much. If he was referring to himself, it seems reasonable to think he actually died from the stoning; and God allowed him to get a glimpse of heaven before restoring his life.

The next day, he departed with Barnabas and went to Derbe. They preached there and made many disciples. Then they did a remarkable thing. They went back through Lystra, Iconium, and Antioch, exhorting the disciples in each place to continue in the faith. Then they appointed elders in each church and fasted and prayed with them before continuing their journey. It took great courage to return to those places where some wanted Paul dead, but he and Barnabas were not harassed any further. God was with them. Perhaps they were able to slip in and out secretly.

They retraced their steps to Perga, and after preaching the word there, they made their way to Attalia, where they were able to go aboard a ship sailing to Antioch. At Antioch, they reported to the church all that God had done through them as He opened the door of faith for the Gentiles to enter the Kingdom of God. It was the end of a very successful missionary tour that resulted in many people turning to the Lord and several churches being established. They started churches in Cyprus, Antioch, Iconium, Lystra, Derbe, and perhaps in Perga.

Discussion Questions
Chapter 12

1. What is it that makes some people ready to accept the truth while others are disposed to reject it?

2. Is it a temptation for us to think too highly of ourselves, to look down on those who are not Christians?

3. How can we develop a love for the lost that will help us think of them as possible brothers and sisters?

4. Do you think Paul was dead after the stoning and was raised by God so he could continue his work?

5. How important is it for us to be the best example we can be for the benefit of those we serve? Can you tell a story of how the genuine faith of someone influenced your life?

6. How important were your parents in leading you to faith in Jesus?

Chapter 13

The Crisis over the Law

"And certain men came down from Judea and taught the brethren, 'Unless you are circumcised according to the custom of Moses, you cannot be saved.' Therefore, when Paul and Barnabas had no small dissension and dispute with them, they determined that Paul and Barnabas and certain others of them should go up to Jerusalem, to the apostles and elders, about this question." **Acts 15:1-2**

The fifteenth chapter of Acts tells the story of the first great crisis inside the church. It tells about how they decided the matter; and how they proceeded after a decision was made. It all started when some men from Judea came to Antioch and began teaching that Gentiles would have to be circumcised and keep the Law to be saved. Paul and Barnabas disagreed and disputed with them about it. The church decided to send Paul, Barnabas, and some others to Jerusalem to consult with the other apostles about it. James, the brother of Jesus, was included in the leadership of the church in Jerusalem at that time. In fact, he seems to have been the one in charge when the leaders met with the congregation to let them know what God's will was in the matter.

Since the overwhelming majority of Christians today are Gentiles, the answer is of great importance to us as it was to them. When they arrived in Jerusalem, they reported on their missions to the Gentile world. After they had completed their report, those who held the opinion that the observance of the law was also required of the Gentiles stated their belief. As a result, the apostles and elders met to discuss the matter. The description of what took place in that meeting gives every appearance of a well-planned meeting.

The first to speak was the apostle, Peter. He reminded them of how God had chosen him to be the first to present the gospel to Gentiles in the home of Cornelius. Jesus had told Peter that He would give him the keys to the kingdom. He unlocked the doors to the kingdom for the Jews on that first Pentecost and for the Gentiles at the home of Cornelius. Peter told the assembly how God had shown His acceptance of Gentiles into His kingdom by pouring out the Holy Spirit on them just as He had on the apostles in the beginning. He went on to point out that God would extend His grace to them just as He had to the Jews.

When Peter finished speaking, Barnabas and Paul told how God had with many miracles and wonders showed His approval of their ministry among the Gentiles.

Then James, who seems to have been presiding at the meeting, spoke. He pointed out that the Scriptures had predicted a time when the Gentiles would be drawn into the kingdom. The passage he quotes is from Amos 9:11,12.

> "After this I will return
> And will rebuild the tabernacle of David, which has fallen;
> I will rebuild its ruins,
> And I will set it up;
> So that the rest of mankind may seek the Lord,
> Even all the Gentiles who are called by My name,
> Says the Lord who does all these things."

At that point, James announced the decision. The apostles had always known the will of God. The Holy Spirit had guided them into all truth as

Jesus had promised (John 16:13). They announced it in this way to settle any question the people had. The decision was unanimous; all the apostles and elders agreed. It was settled once and for all.

These facts are further established by what Paul wrote to the Galatians in chapter two, verses six through sixteen. First, the gospel preached to the Gentiles by Paul and Barnabas was the same as what Peter and the others preached among the Jews (Acts 15:6-10). Second, "We believe that through the grace of the Lord Jesus Christ we shall be saved in the same manner as they." Paul reaffirms that truth in Galatians 2:16, "A man is not justified by the works of the law but by faith in Jesus Christ, even we have believed in Christ Jesus, that we might be justified by faith in Christ and not by the works of the law; for by the works of the law no flesh shall be justified."

Two other facts are given by Paul in Galatians. The first is that this trip was fourteen years after the trip he made there after his conversion. The second is the fact that He went to Jerusalem at that time because the Lord had revealed that it was His will that Paul go.

I want to get back to the core problem that made this meeting necessary. Paul says in Galatians 2:4, "And this occurred because of false brethren secretly brought in (who came in by stealth to spy out our liberty which we have in Christ Jesus, that they might bring us into bondage.)" He was talking about the bondage of the Law of Moses. If they had succeeded, the Gentiles would have been required to become Jews before they could enter the Kingdom of God. The church would then have become just another sect of Judaism. It would have been a disaster for the church. This decision completely separated the church from Judaism forever.

A copy of the letter sent to the Gentile churches is printed below.

"The apostles, the elders, and the brethren,

To the brethren who are of the Gentiles in Antioch, Syria, and Cilicia:

Greetings.

Since we have heard that some who went out from us have troubled you with words, unsettling your souls, saying, 'You must be circumcised and keep the law'—to whom we gave no such commandment— it seemed good to us, being assembled with one accord, to send chosen men to you with our beloved Barnabas and Paul, men who have risked their lives for the name of our Lord Jesus Christ. We have therefore sent Judas and Silas, who will also report the same things by word of mouth. For it seemed good to the Holy Spirit, and to us, to lay upon you no greater burden than these necessary things: that you abstain from things offered to idols, from blood, from things strangled, and from sexual immorality. If you keep yourselves from these, you will do well.

Farewell." Acts 15:23-29

It was a simple, straightforward letter that informed them that they were not required to keep the Law. It told them of the only provisions of the law which they would be required to obey.

Those are still binding for Christians today. We have no right to alter or change what God has unmistakably commanded. We cannot exclude anyone from our fellowship based on their race, nationality, color, or economic status. All who believe, repent, confess their faith, and submit to baptism in the name of the Father, His Son, and the Holy Spirit, have entered the kingdom. Our part is to welcome them and do all we can to help them grow in Christ.

Whenever we disagree with the church, our elders should handle it as they did. Let those who have a grievance bring it into the open, search the scriptures to determine God's will. Fast and pray to seek God's will on the matter, show the people that it has been interpreted correctly, and announce their decision. Make sure the people understand why they reached the decision, and that they must abide by that decision.

If every church followed this plan, we would avoid many disputes, and divisions could be prevented.

Two Separate Missionary Endeavors

"Then after some days Paul said to Barnabas, 'Let us now go back and visit our brethren in every city where we have preached the word of the Lord, and see how they are doing.' Now Barnabas was determined to take with them John called Mark. But Paul insisted that they should not take with them the one who had departed from them in Pamphylia, and had not gone with them to the work. Then the contention became so sharp that they parted from one another. And so Barnabas took Mark and sailed to Cyprus; but Paul chose Silas and departed, being commended by the brethren to the grace of God. And he went through Syria and Cilicia, strengthening the churches." Acts 15:36-41

When the meeting in Jerusalem was over, Paul and Barnabas headed back to Antioch with the letter explaining that Gentiles would not be required to obey the Law of Moses in order to be a part of the church. They were accompanied by Silas and Judas from the Jerusalem church, who were sent to confirm that the letter was indeed from the apostles and elders in Jerusalem. The apostles were unanimous in their decision. They required only purity in the lives of converts from pagan religion. Purity meant abstaining from all kinds of sexual sins, which include all sex outside of marriage between a man and a woman. Purity also included not eating meat with blood, including meat from animals that had been strangled, since the blood would not have been drained. It also included meat that had been rendered unclean because it had been offered in sacrifice to idols. Paul later clarified this restriction by indicating that it was not necessary to ask about the meat you were being served or what was bought in the meat market. He taught that it was permissible to eat such meat with a good conscience. (1 Corinthians 10:25-27)

After a period of some days, Paul suggested to Barnabas that they return to the churches they had established to see how they were doing. Barnabas was all for the trip and suggested they take John Mark with them again. Paul objected. He thought Mark could not be trusted to stick with them. Their disagreement resulted in the two missionaries breaking up their partnership. Barnabas took JohnMark and left for Cyprus. Paul took Silas and headed for the churches they had established in Lycaonia, Lystra, and Derbe. We know about Paul's success, but not much about Barnabas from this time forward. We do know that Mark overcame his early weakness. He became a co-worker with Peter and wrote the gospel of Mark. Paul's opinion changed. He wrote kindly about him in 2 Timothy 4:11, "Only Luke is with me. Get Mark and bring him with you, for he is useful to me for ministry."

There are some valuable lessons to be learned from this episode in the life of Paul and Barnabas. The first is that the greatest and best men make mistakes. They sin.

Perhaps Paul and Barnabas both sinned in this incident. At first, Paul tried to convince Barnabas that it would not be wise to take Mark with them the second time, but he may have ended up saying some unkind things that were hurtful to Barnabas. On the other hand, Barnabas was so determined to take Mark that he also said some things he regretted. I am speculating here. Perhaps they parted without unkind words. Perhaps they each wished the other the best in their further endeavors.

If they sinned, their sins were brought on by the very things that made them great. Paul's intensity and his great zeal that drove him to always give the best simply could not endure anything that even appeared to be half-hearted service. The gentle, loving soul of Barnabas led him to be less demanding and more tolerant of weakness in his companions.

This story illustrates how good people sometimes don't recognize their own faults. Frank and Eddie Dudley grew up poor. After he finished college, Frank moved to New York, started an advertising agency, and became rather wealthy. His brother, Eddie, became a college professor. One afternoon, Frank travelled to Boston and checked into a hotel room. He then called Eddie's house. When Eddie's wife Agnes answered, he invited her and Eddie to have dinner with him. Agnes replied that she was sorry, but Eddie had a meeting that night, and she also had a conflict. She went on to say she would have Eddie call when he got home. Sometime later, Eddie called and suggested they have lunch together the next day. Frank accepted; and they ended the call. Later that night, another friend told him Eddie was having a party and suggested he would see him there.

The next day, Frank went to Eddie's house. When Agnes came to the door, he blurted out, "Why did you lie to me about last night?" Agnes told him it was a special night for Eddie. The president of the college was there; and they hoped he would tell Eddie he was getting a promotion. "You would have ruined everything," she said. You always have to show Eddie up. You have to tell a better story. You always make Eddie feel inferior." "But I'm not like that at all," Frank replied, "How can you say that?" "Aren't you," Agnes said, "You need to take a good look at yourself."

Frank was furious, but he decided to do what she suggested. Over the next several days, he always stopped himself when he was about to speak in a group. He discovered Agnes was right. He always had to be the best in any conversation.

Not long after that, Frank went to Eddie's house again. Agnes was reluctant to let him in, but she did. Frank was carrying a simple wrapped package. It was a birthday present for little Eddie, his brother's son. He had planned to give the boy an expensive watch, but then he realized it was far more expensive than anything Eddie could give his son, so he brought a plain book with a black cover. He explained to little Eddie that it was a scrapbook he had been compiling over the years. There were pictures of Eddie when he was a track star in high school, and several notes from different people who were expressing their hopes and prayers for Eddie when he was missing during World War II. One note said, "You have a brilliant mind, but your brother Eddie has a generous soul; and that is much better." "Who sent you that?" asked little Eddie. "My second best friend in the world," Frank answered. "Who is your best friend in the world?" the boy asked. Frank said, "You see that lady over there," indicating Agnes. "Your best friend will tell you what you need to hear even when you don't want to hear it."

Agnes did something she had never done before. She came over, put her arms around Frank, and gave him a sisterly kiss. By Fulton Oursler

The scriptures do not hide the faults of great men of God but record them for our learning. All people sin; even the greatest fail at times. We do not need to think of ourselves as totally unworthy creatures. With the help of the Holy Spirit, we can overcome our weaknesses and become valuable servants of the Lord. God does not reject a man because of one momentary lapse into old habits. He looks at a man in a more comprehensive way. He knows if we are generally walking paths of righteousness; and He is always willing to forgive when we repent. We should look at people in the same way. We should not allow their imperfections to turn us against them. Rather, we should love them and consider their sins temporary deviations from the paths of righteousness.

God can achieve great results even when we make bad mistakes. Consider the case of John Mark. He had abandoned Paul and Barnabas on the first missionary journey. Would he have done that if he had realized that his weakness would eventually separate Paul and Barnabas? He needed the harshness of Paul to make him take a good look at himself. We never know what impact our sins may have on others. On the other hand, he needed the gentleness of Barnabas to keep him from feeling deserted. He developed into a valuable coworker under the leadership of Barnabas.

Consider what happened in regard to the mission work. Instead of one team going out to spread the gospel, there were two. Another valuable servant was brought on board to help with the work. Paul and Silas were successful missionaries. They preached the gospel and established churches for many years. Barnabas and Mark were also successful.

We don't know how much more could have been accomplished if they had continued to work together. Men of God can disagree and still get along. Love can work to find a middle ground. In matters of less importance, one can simply give in and go along with the other person's idea. Either Paul or Barnabas could have said, "I can't agree with you on this. If you want to go in one direction, I'll go in another. We will ask God to bless both of our endeavors."

Discussion Questions
Chapter 13

1. Do you think those who wanted to require Gentiles to observe the Law of Moses were satisfied with the decision of the apostles and elders? What evidence do you have to support your view?

2. Who do you think was right about taking Mark, Paul, or Barnabas? Why?

3. Do we ever miss the real solution to a problem because we stubbornly hang onto our opinion?

4. Do you think Paul was driven to do more because he had fought against the church in the beginning?

5. Do you think we go too easy on our children instead of expecting more from them?

Chapter 14

The Power of Example

"Then he came to Derbe and Lystra. And behold, a certain disciple was there, named Timothy, the son of a certain Jewish woman who believed, but his father was Greek. He was well spoken of by the brethren who were at Lystra and Iconium. Paul wanted to have him go on with him. And he took him and circumcised him because of the Jews who were in that region, for they all knew that his father was Greek. And as they went through the cities, they delivered to them the decrees to keep, which were determined by the apostles and elders at Jerusalem. So the churches were strengthened in the faith, and increased in number daily." **Acts 16:1-5**

It's easier to follow a person than to follow his instructions. That's why it is so important to make sure we set a good example, sometimes people don't even realize they are copying someone they admire. I once knew a young preacher who had copied his college professor so well that anyone could guess where he had gone to school.

Children almost always copy their parents. Sometimes they say something that makes it quite clear where they got it. One time my wife had a problem in the kitchen. Her pressure cooker had blown its safety valve and sprayed the liquid from inside all over the ceiling and the walls. Our little daughter, who was about four years old at the time, came into the kitchen, placed her hands on her hips and asked, "Who's responsible for this mess?" Do you think she had heard that from her mother?

Preachers should always keep in mind this little poem,

I'd rather see a sermon than hear one any day. I'd rather one walk beside me than simply point the way.

God of course, understands the power and appeal of example. One reason Jesus came into the world was to show us how to live to please God. The Bible is full of examples of godly men and women. We learn as much or more from their examples as we do from their teachings. The early church is also described in the Bible so that we might follow its example in many things. In our text for today, we can see examples that show us how to serve the Lord as parents, as a church, and as leaders in the church.

Let's talk about the example of parents and grandparents. Here in Acts 16:1-3, Luke tells us about Timothy. When Paul wanted him to join their company, he had him circumcised because his mother was Jewish, but his father was Greek. He knew the Jews would be offended if he had not followed that law. Timothy had been doing some preaching in the area and was well respected by the people.

Titus was another young man who worked with Paul. He had no Jewish heritage, so Paul insisted he need not be circumcised. He would not give in at all.

In 2 Timothy 1:5, Paul speaks of the genuine faith that was in Timothy's mother and grandmother. They had taught him the scriptures when he was a child. By doing that, they had laid a foundation that prepared him to accept the gospel.

Parents have a responsibility to their children, which they sometimes neglect. We take care of their physical needs for food, clothing, and shelter. We take care of their social and economic needs. We send them to school or homeschool them. We teach them manners and what is appropriate in different situations, but we expect the church to take care of their spiritual needs. In Deuteronomy 6:6-9, the Lord says to His people, "And these words which I command you today shall be in your heart. You shall teach them diligently to your children, and shall talk of them when you sit in your house, when you walk by the way, when you lie down, and when you rise. You shall bind them as a sign on your hand, and they shall be as frontlets between your eyes. You shall write them on the doorposts of your house and on your gates." The meaning is obvious. God wants us to keep his words in the forefront of our minds and those of our children. The Jews took this commandment literally. They tied little boxes on their wrist with scripture verses in them. They wrote them on their houses. We would do well to decorate our houses with pictures containing our favorite scriptures. Our children need to see how important the Bible is to us. We should read it every day with our families and discuss its meaning and how to apply it in our daily lives.

The early church encouraged and developed young men in the faith. The fact that the scripture says Timothy was well reported of by the brethren shows that they were talking about him and saying encouraging things. Young people blossom when you give them a pat on the back. The church trusted Timothy and gave him jobs to do. He responded positively.

Too often, we think no one else can do a job as well as we do, so we are reluctant to give them responsibility. They will never grow to fulfill their potential unless we trust them. Young people should be encouraged to go to Bible college. There is no happier life than that which is found in serving the Lord. They can build happy marriages and satisfying lives if they put Jesus first. In addition, there is no more important work in the world. They will learn to build a life, not just how to earn a living.

We must show by example the joy of sacrificing for others. There is nothing that makes one feel good about themselves like doing something that costs us something to benefit others. I remember one time when I was a child asking my mother why people don't do more for others, because it makes you feel so good. A lady who led children's worship one time asked the children to bring their favorite toy to church to give to other children who wouldn't have anything for Christmas. I'm sure some of them did it. I suppose some parents said, "You don't have to give your favorite. One of your other toys will do." If they did that, they deprived their children of the joy of going the extra mile for others. I will always remember a thing that happened in the first little church where I preached. Almost all of the families in that church were "sharecroppers." They worked a portion of land that belonged to someone else and received a share of the crops for their labor. They were very poor. They lived in shacks that we wouldn't keep our pets in. When the father of one of those families got sick and couldn't work, the other families brought food to help them out. These people had so little, yet they gave so much. No one brought just a few cans. They brought home canned vegetables, not just a few, but large boxes full of a dozen or more pints and quarts of food. I have never seen more prosperous people give as those people did. If I were to give an amount to a food drive today, that is, considering what I make today, it would be more than a hundred dollars' worth of food. And I am living on Social Security. Their generosity was inspiring and humbling.

Paul and Silas maintained the highest ethical standards. They delivered the decrees to all of the churches, even those that didn't need them, because that was what they were sent to do. We must be scrupulous about living up to the highest ethical standards. Give a full day's labor for a full day's pay. Make sure our language is free from profanity. Be generous. If someone else provides a car to take your children to church camp, give them money for gas, even if your children are not going. Do your fair share and more.

Paul and Silas spent their time strengthening and encouraging the Christians as well as seeking the lost. They taught the whole counsel of God. They trusted them with jobs they could handle. They made them feel needed. They loved them genuinely and showed it.

To be the leaders God wants us to be, we must teach our children the way of the Lord. We must be good examples for them. As church leaders, we must encourage all to get involved in the work of the kingdom of God, maintain the highest ethical standards, be generous and sacrifice for others, do all we can to encourage and strengthen others in the faith, visit and care for the sick, widows, orphans, and all who are in need.

Jesus provided the perfect example for us to follow. We must always seek to walk in His footsteps.

Come Help Us

"Now when they had gone through Phrygia and the region of Galatia, they were forbidden by the Holy Spirit to preach the word in Asia. After they had come to Mysia, they tried to go into Bithynia, but the Spirit did not permit them. So passing by Mysia, they came down to Troas. And a vision appeared to Paul in the night. A man of Macedonia stood and pleaded with him, saying, "Come over to Macedonia and help us." Now after he had seen the vision, immediately we sought to go to Macedonia, concluding that the Lord had called us to preach the gospel to them." Acts 16:6-10

This passage tells a remarkable story, the story of a pagan asking Christian evangelists to come and help them. We know it was a vision, and the person in the vision only represented a society without Christ, as such, it represents a real concern in the non-Christian world. They have no real hope. Their only hope is that this life is all there is, that when they close their eyes in death, they cease to exist. In Christ, we have a wonderful hope that is more than a hope. It is the assurance that our hope will be realized. We will live again in paradise; and that life will never end. A never-ending life in paradise. A perfect life in the presence of our Father and our Savior.

The pagan world lives in darkness. It is a life of superstition and fear, a life with no purpose higher than self. If they knew of the hope and joy of the Christian life, they would certainly say, "Come! Help us!"

The opportunities to accomplish great things in the field of worldwide evangelism have never been greater than they are today. There are approximately 8 billion people in the world today. Something like one half of them don't know about Jesus. Many of them live in atrocious conditions in India, Africa, and Asia. We have the ability to take the message of hope to them.

Christians in America don't appreciate how incredibly wealthy we are. Do you know that Jesus owned nothing but the clothes on His back when He died? The lictors who crucified him had the right to confiscate His belongings. They divided His garments among them because there was nothing else to seize. The poorest among us have a change of clothing. The homeless among us are mostly drug addicts and drunks. There are those who are living in their cars, but most of those living on the streets of our cities are there because of what they have done to themselves.

If we count the number of families who are active members in the Christian churches and Churches of Christ in America, the total would be nearly one million families. If they gave an average of ten dollars a week for the spread of the gospel message throughout the world, it would amount to about $250 million a year. We could print Bibles in every language, broadcast the gospel by television to every country in the world, and saturate the radio waves all over the world with the gospel. We could see to it that everyone had access to the gospel in a very short time. We lack only the commitment to get the job done.

We are not doing it because we don't care enough. That is a terrible indictment, but it is true. What other explanation could there be? We have ignored the orders of our commander-in-chief in Matthew 28:18-20. Jesus said, "Go ye therefore and teach all nations, baptizing them in the name of the Father and of the Son and of the Holy Spirit, teaching them to observe all things whatsoever I have commanded you, and lo, I am with you always, even to the end of the world." In Mark 16:15-16, Mark records it a little differently. He tells us to "Go into all the world and preach the gospel to every creature." I'm sure Jesus said both of those things on different occasions. He also told the apostles, "You shall receive power when the Holy Spirit has come upon you; and you shall be witnesses to Me in Jerusalem, and in all Judea and Samaria, and to the end of the earth." (Acts 1:8)

The responsibility of taking the gospel into all the world was not only given to the apostles. It falls on all of us as well. If we fail to accept that responsibility, we will be held accountable. The Lord warned Ezekiel about shirking his responsibility; and His warning applies to us as well. "When I say to the wicked, 'You shall surely die,' and you give him no warning, nor speak to warn the wicked from his wicked way, to save his life, that same wicked man shall die in his iniquity; but his blood I will require at your hand. Yet, if you warn the wicked, and he does not turn from his wickedness, nor from his wicked way, he shall die in his iniquity; but you have delivered your soul" (Ezekiel 3:18-19).

When the Lord Jesus told the story of the good Samaritan, the point was simple. The priest and the Levite did not care enough about the injured man to give their time and resources to help him. The Samaritan cared for his neighbor more than he cared for his time and money. If we don't have that kind of compassion, how could we say we are followers of Jesus? I believe most of us would stop to help someone who had been attacked and left half dead. We would do much the same as the Samaritan did. Yet, there are billions of people in this world who don't know Jesus loves them and wants to save them. Why don't we care as much for their souls as we care for an injured man at the side of the road? Could it be that we don't really think they will die in their sins if they don't learn about Him? Is it that they are far away, and since we don't see them, we don't think about them? I think it is this last thing that keeps us from sacrificing to get the word to them. "Out of sight, out of mind." God cared enough about them to send His Son to die for them. He must be very disappointed in us because we don't really care that much.

I wonder if someone is reading this right now who cares enough to say, "I'll go! Send me!" Perhaps someone will say, "I don't really need that new car. I'll give what it would have cost me to send someone to tell them about Jesus." Maybe someone will decide to skip a vacation this year and give that money to spread the gospel message. How much do we really care? I started to write, "How much do you care?" Then I realized I needed to ask myself that question too.

We have the technology to let the whole world know about the Savior. We have the money to put a piece of literature into the hands of every person in the world. Why don't we do it? Are we so focused on ourselves that we are willing to let others perish? Do we need to repent?

Preaching in Europe

"Therefore, sailing from Troas, we ran a straight course to Samothrace, and the next day came to Neapolis, and from there to Philippi, which is the foremost city of that part of Macedonia, a colony. And we were staying in that city for some days. And on the Sabbath day we went out of the city to the riverside, where prayer was customarily made; and we sat down and spoke to the women who met there. Now a certain woman named Lydia heard us. She was a seller of purple from the city of Thyatira, who worshiped God. The Lord opened her heart to heed the things spoken by Paul. And when she and her household were baptized, she begged us, saying, 'If you have judged me to be faithful to the Lord, come to my house and stay.' So she persuaded us." Acts 16:11-15

After encouraging and strengthening the churches in Lystra, Derbe, Iconium, and Antioch, Paul and Silas made their way to Troas. There, Paul had a vision of a man from Macedonia saying, "Come over to Macedonia and help us." They sailed from Troas and soon came to Macedonia and made their way to Philippi. They did not find a synagogue there but discovered there was a place of worship beside the River Gangites just outside the city. They made their way to the place on the Sabbath day and preached the gospel to the people gathered there. Among those present was the family of a businesswoman from Thyatira named Lydia. It was the first time the gospel was preached in Europe. Lydia and her family believed and were baptized.

This story, along with others of whole families being baptized, has been used by some to justify infant baptism, but no one can prove there were any children in her household. There is no indication that she was married. Her household would have been made up of those who were her servants. The customs and prejudices of the times probably meant that the members of her household were all females.

Lydia's business was selling purple garments and/or cloth. Murex sea snails native to the Mediterranean Sea were the primary source of the rare and highly prized Tyrian purple dye produced in ancient Phoenicia. The dye was extracted from a gland in the snail that secretes mucus that turns into an intense purple color when exposed to sunlight. Because of the difficulty of producing this dye, it was very expensive, and thus it was called royal purple. There were three plant sources that were used to create purple dye: madder root, sawwort, and lichens. Plant-based purple had more red in it than the royal purple. It was easier to produce and was, therefore, not as expensive as the royal purple.

The city of Thyatira was Lydia's home. It was a source of the purple dye made from plants. It was most likely the purple that Lydia sold. There was a much broader market for it since only the wealthiest people could afford the royal purple.

The fact that Lydia and her household observed the Sabbath in a city without a synagogue is a testament to her genuine devotion to God. It is not surprising that the Lord rewarded her faith by sending Paul and Silas to share the gospel message with her and her devout household. The fourteenth verse of Acts sixteen tells us the Lord opened Lydia's heart to heed the things spoken by Paul. There was no special blessing from the Lord that opened her heart. It was the same process that works in all hearts of those who obey the gospel. She heard the gospel message, and through it, the Holy Spirit led her to accept it by faith.

It is interesting to see how small, seemingly insignificant things may prove to be of tremendous importance. Who would have expected that this small gathering of people on the banks of a river in Macedonia could be the beginning of a movement that swept across Europe and changed the course of history? Idolatry was abandoned as Europeans embraced the gospel. Christianity would overcome the power of Rome, confound the philosophies of Athens, and turn the hearts of the people from gross sensuality to the pure and holy living Jesus taught. Europe became the champion and chief disseminator of the gospel. Almost everything that has benefited modern man was produced by these people once they were enlightened by the gospel. Of course, God knew all of this would happen. It is, no doubt, the reason He gave Paul the vision which led him to Macedonia. It all started with a small group of dedicated women meeting on the bank of a river to worship God.

We should take this incident as both a challenge and a warning. What if Paul had decided to turn back to Asia after finding there was no synagogue in Philippi? He believed he was in the right place because God had led him there. He used one small opportunity to begin a movement in Europe that would change the world. Who knows if the person you work besides, or the person who moves in next door, or the person of a different race who visits your church, may be the one who will have an impact far beyond your imagination. Every one of those scenarios has taken place in my ministry, and each of them resulted in great blessings in my work.

Think of some examples in the Bible. Andrew brought his brother Peter to Jesus. Barnabas believed in Paul and brought him to Antioch to work with him there and later partnered with him to take the gospel to the Gentiles. He also mentored Mark, who started poorly but ended up writing one of the gospels in the New Testament. You may meet someone today who could be the next great leader in the church. Do not neglect the opportunity to lead that person to Jesus. One day, we will stand before the Lord to give an account of what we have done or failed to do.

God has not called us to some great work that will bring us fame and fortune. He has called us to be faithful in the smallest things. He has asked us to be servants. He may turn your small act of kindness or your quiet conversation with an unbeliever into a moment that will change the world. Let us give ourselves to the tasks at hand with sincerity and fervor. God will take care of the results.

Our work for Jesus will be of eternal significance. Long after the names of great athletes have faded from memory, when all the names of powerful politicians have been forgotten, our names will shine in eternity if we have just been faithful.

The Philippian Jailer

"Now it happened, as we went to prayer, that a certain slave girl possessed with a spirit of divination met us, who brought her masters much profit by fortune-telling. This girl followed Paul and us, and cried out, saying, 'These men are the servants of the Most High God, who proclaim to us the way of salvation.' And this she did for many days.

But Paul, greatly annoyed, turned and said to the spirit, 'I command you in the name of Jesus Christ to come out of her.' And he came out that very hour. But when her masters saw that their hope of profit was gone, they seized Paul and Silas and dragged them into the marketplace to the authorities.

And they brought them to the magistrates, and said, 'These men, being Jews, exceedingly trouble our city; and they teach customs which are not lawful for us, being Romans, to receive or observe.' Then the multitude rose together against them; and the magistrates tore off their clothes and commanded them to be beaten with rods. And when they had laid many stripes on them, they threw them into prison, commanding the jailer to keep them securely. Having received such a charge, he put them into the inner prison and fastened their feet in the stocks.

But at midnight, Paul and Silas were praying and singing hymns to God, and the prisoners were listening to them. Suddenly, there was a great earthquake, so that the foundations of the prison were shaken; and immediately all the doors were opened and everyone's chains were loosed. And the keeper of the prison, awaking from sleep and seeing the prison doors open, supposing the prisoners had fled, drew his sword and was about to kill himself. But Paul called with a loud voice, saying, 'Do yourself no harm, for we are all here.'

Then he called for a light, ran in, and fell trembling before Paul and Silas. And he brought them out and said, 'Sirs, what must I do to be saved?'

So they said, 'Believe on the Lord Jesus Christ, and you will be saved, you and your household.' Then they spoke the word of the Lord to him and to all who were in his house. And he took them the same hour of the night and washed their stripes. And immediately he and all his family were baptized. Now when he had brought them into his house, he set food before them; and he rejoiced, having believed in God with all his household." Acts 16:16-34

The Bible is very helpful in guiding our daily lives because it gives us more than abstract principles. It gives us concrete examples of people who either applied properly or misapplied those principles. Many times, we find it much easier to follow an example. We can easily see the consequences of failing to properly apply those principles in our daily lives.

The story of Paul and Silas being arrested and the way they reacted to that arrest is a great example of what I am talking about. It shows us what Satan produces in the lives of worldly men. They are self-centered, callous individuals who care only for themselves. The misery of the slave girl who was possessed by a demon meant nothing to her owners. They cared only for the money they could make from her. It sounds horrible, yet there is a modern equivalent in sex slavery, and many of the victims are underage girls. Some of them are small children. Any decent human being finds this unimaginably depraved, yet there is a ready market for these slaves. Human beings can be incredibly cruel.

After the conversion of Lydia's household, Paul and Silas apparently continued to go to the place of prayer by the river. As they were going to pray, a slave girl began following them every day. She was possessed by an evil spirit, which enabled her to be a fortune teller. The evil spirit spoke through her, saying, "These men are servants of the Most High God, who proclaim to us the way of salvation." Paul and Silas were greatly annoyed because they did not want people to associate them with the evil spirit, so Paul spoke to the spirit and commanded it in the name of Jesus Christ to come out of her. The spirit immediately obeyed. One result of its departure was that the slave girl could no longer tell fortunes. Her owners were infuriated that their source of revenue was gone, so they brought charges against Paul and Silas. The charges concealed the real reason they wanted them arrested, which was a desire for revenge. They said, "These men, being Jews, exceedingly trouble our city; and they teach customs which are not lawful for us, being Romans, to receive or observe" (Acts 16:20-21).

The authorities had them severely beaten and thrown into jail. The jailer put them into the inner prison and fastened their feet in stocks. What happened next is astonishing and inspiring. Paul and Silas demonstrated the amazing serenity of children of God. They were praying and singing praises to God at midnight; and the other prisoners were listening. They must have been amazed. The worst conditions are accepted by Christians with a calm and joyous spirit because they are suffering for their Savior. Their attitudes and actions bring glory to the name of the Lord.

Suddenly, a great earthquake shook the foundation of the prison, the doors flew open, and every prisoner's chains fell off. The jailer's reaction is understandable when you realize the Romans would execute anyone who allowed his prisoners to escape. When the jailer saw all the prison doors open, he was about to kill himself when he heard Paul's voice calling out, "Do yourself no harm, for we are all here" (Acts 16:28). Now, I don't know why none of the prisoners tried to escape. Perhaps they were in shock, or maybe they wanted to hear about the God who had set them free.

When the jailer asked Paul and Silas, "What must I do to be saved?" they answered, "Believe on the Lord Jesus Christ, and you will be saved, you and your household" (Acts 16:30-31). The question immediately comes to mind, "Why is this answer so different from the one Peter gave to the same question in Acts 2:38?" He told the people that day to repent and be baptized for the remission of their sins. Why doesn't Paul give the jailer the same answer? The correct answer is that the people in the temple on Pentecost were in a different place spiritually than the jailer. They already believed in the Lord Jesus. They were ready for the next step. The jailer didn't know about Jesus and God's plan to save his soul, so Paul told him where to start, assuming he would follow through with the next steps when he believed. His assumption was correct because the jailer washed and treated their beaten backs, demonstrating his repentance, and was immediately baptized with his whole household. (Acts 16:33) Please note that Paul and Silas spoke the word to them, thereby giving them further instructions concerning the additional things they would need to do to claim the salvation Jesus was offering them. (Acts 16:32)

The contrast between the slave masters and the missionaries couldn't be more obvious. The slave masters were self-serving, thoughtless, cruel, and vindictive. They cared only for themselves. They didn't give a thought to the awful, mind-numbing possession the girl was living in. They exploited her condition for their own profit; and they wanted revenge when Paul and Silas showed compassion toward the girl. The missionaries, on the other hand, cared about the girl. They set her free from her bondage to the evil spirit. They showed the joy in their lives when they were singing and praying at midnight. They shared that joy with the jailer and his family. Finally, they protected the reputation of the Lord by not allowing their persecutors to slink away after the shameful way they treated the apostles. They required a public release from prison.

The superiority of the Christian life is on full display in the sixteenth chapter of Acts. To the non-Christian, the reaction of Paul and Silas after they were beaten and fastened in stocks must seem incredible. How could anyone in such pain and misery pray and sing in the inner prison? You might say dungeon. It was probably dark and damp and rat-infested.

Paul and Silas lived in joy and peace that outward circumstances could not destroy. They experienced joy because they knew their Father in heaven loved them and would welcome them into heaven when they died. Circumstances are temporary. Heaven is eternal. Their inner peace was produced by the knowledge that their sins had been forgiven. There was no guilt to harass them because they had been set free from the burden of guilt by the blood of the Lamb of God.

Joni Eareckson was injured in a diving accident when she was seventeen years old. She was permanently paralyzed from the neck down. She learned to draw, holding the pencil in her teeth, and soon began producing greeting cards. Later, she wrote a book about her experiences. In 1982, she married Ken Tada. They are still together after more than forty-two years. She is a vibrant, vivacious, joyful person because of her relationship with Jesus.

Peace that surpasses understanding and joy unspeakable are available to all who follow Jesus through faith and obedience. Outward circumstances cannot take our peace and joy away.

Discussion Questions
Chapter 14

1. Do you think it was common for Jews to find a quiet place to worship if there was no synagogue in a city?

2. Why do you think it never mentions a husband for Lydia? Do you think she made Philippi her permanent home? Why or why not?

3. Why do you think the demon that possessed the slave girl had her proclaiming that Paul and Silas were servants of the Most High God?

4. Why did Paul insist that the authorities release them publicly?

5. Why is it that many Christians in America don't have the peace Paul and Silas had?

Chapter 15

The Faith Paul Preached

"Now when they had passed through Amphipolis and Apollonia, they came to Thessalonica, where there was a synagogue of the Jews. Then Paul, as his custom was, went in to them, and for three Sabbaths reasoned with them from the Scriptures, explaining and demonstrating that the Christ had to suffer and rise again from the dead, and saying, 'This Jesus whom I preach to you is the Christ.' And some of them were persuaded; and a great multitude of the devout Greeks, and not a few of the leading women, joined Paul and Silas.

But the Jews who were not persuaded, becoming envious, took some of the evil men from the marketplace, and gathering a mob, set all the city in an uproar and attacked the house of Jason, and sought to bring them out to the people. But when they did not find them, they dragged Jason and some brethren to the rulers of the city, crying out, 'These who have turned the world upside down have come here too. Jason has harbored them, and these are all acting contrary to the decrees of Caesar, saying there is another king—Jesus.' And they troubled the crowd and the rulers of the city when they heard these things. So when they had taken security from Jason and the rest, they let them go.

Then the brethren immediately sent Paul and Silas away by night to Berea. When they arrived, they went into the synagogue of the Jews. These were more fair-minded than those in Thessalonica, in that they received the word with all readiness, and searched the Scriptures daily to find out whether these things were so. Therefore many of them believed, and also not a few of the Greeks, prominent women as well as men. But when the Jews from Thessalonica learned that the word of God was preached by Paul at Berea, they came there also and stirred up the crowds. Then immediately the brethren sent Paul away, to go to the sea; but both Silas and Timothy remained there. So those who conducted Paul brought him to Athens; and receiving a command for Silas and Timothy to come to him with all speed, they departed." **Acts 17:1-15**

When Paul came to town, things happened. Look at what happened everywhere he went in Macedonia. In Philippi, they led Lydia and her household to the faith in Jesus. They healed a slave girl who was possessed by a demon. They were beaten and thrown into jail. They converted the jailer. Then they moved on to Thessalonica. They preached in the synagogue and led a multitude to Christ. The unbelieving Jews stirred up the city and said, "Those who have turned the world upside down have come here also." So, they had to leave town. They moved on to Berea. The synagogue there received them readily and searched the scriptures to confirm what Paul and Silas preached. Then their old foes from Thessalonica came and stirred up the crowds against them. Once again, Paul had to leave town. Everywhere he went in Macedonia, he caused an uproar. When most of us come into town, we don't even get the church stirred up. It certainly would not be called an uproar, more of a whimper. Most of us don't like confrontations, yet we would never convert anyone if we did not confront them with the gospel. I would venture to say that ninety-nine percent of the people who have come to Christ through my ministry did so because I asked them if they would accept Jesus and be baptized. I confronted them with their need to make a decision.

We are going to take a look at the faith Paul preached to see what it was that made him so controversial.

First, he taught that Jesus is the promised Messiah (Acts 17:1-2). He preached that Christ needed to suffer and rise from the dead. The Jews at that time expected the Messiah would overthrow the Roman oppressors and re-establish the throne of David. They expected the kingdom to have all the power and glory of the kingdom under Solomon. The idea of a suffering Savior was the furthest thing from their minds, but Paul showed them that the Old Testament predicted it. Genesis 3:15 includes the earliest prediction of His suffering. Speaking to Satan, God said:

> "And I will put enmity
> Between you and the woman,
> And between your seed and her Seed;
> He shall bruise your head,
> And you shall bruise His heel."

The Messiah would suffer in the process of overcoming Satan. It was a prediction of the suffering of One who would destroy the power of Satan but would be harmed by dying to save the world. Isaiah 53:4-6 says,

> "Surely He has borne our griefs
> And carried our sorrows;
> Yet we esteemed Him stricken,
> Smitten by God, and afflicted.
> But He was wounded for our transgressions,
> He was bruised for our iniquities;
> The chastisement for our peace was upon Him,
> And by His stripes we are healed.
> All we like sheep have gone astray;
> We have turned, every one, to his own way;
> And the Lord has laid on Him the iniquity of us all."

The Old Testament also predicts the resurrection.
"I have set the Lord always before me;
Because He is at my right hand I shall not be moved.
Therefore, my heart is glad, and my glory rejoices;
My flesh also will rest in hope.
For You will not leave my soul in Sheol,
Nor will You allow Your Holy One to see corruption.
You will show me the path of life;
In Your presence is fullness of joy;
At Your right hand are pleasures forevermore."
Psalm 16:8-11

Sheol was the name they gave to the place where the dead await the resurrection and Judgement Day. The Holy One would not remain there, and His body would not decay. He would return to life before the decomposition could begin. Paul preached that Jesus fulfilled those predictions; and that he and the other apostles were eyewitnesses to the resurrection, as were more than five hundred others. Every preacher today should preach that same gospel message. Every Christian should share it.

The message was received by some with joy and gladness. The people of Berea were more fair-minded than many others who heard the gospel message because they searched the scriptures to determine if these things were true. As a result, a large number of them believed and were baptized.

Those who accepted and obeyed the gospel made drastic changes in their lifestyle. For pagans that meant getting rid of everything associated with idolatry. All of their images, their household gods. It meant no more participation in the debauchery associated with idol worship. For those who come to Jesus today it often means a change in their language, in what they watch on TV, in their drinking habits or drug use. It means being kind to all, even our enemies. It means contributing a part of our income to the church, to missions, to the relief of disaster victims, and to missions for the spread of the gospel, and many other manifestations of our love for God and our neighbors.

When Paul and Silas entered a town, they first went to the synagogue to proclaim the message of salvation. The Jews were their best hope of making converts. They had been prepared by their upbringing; and they were looking for the Messiah. Usually opposition arose very quickly; and they had to find another location to meet for worship and observe the Lord's Supper.

We don't have a synagogue in most towns in America. Most of our preaching is done in our churches. In some places, Christian schools give us a chance of reaching out to others in the name of Christ. The one thing we often neglect is house-to-house sharing of the gospel. The apostle Paul spoke to the elders of Ephesus and reminded them of how he taught publicly and from house to house. We need to do more of that. Let us dedicate ourselves to spreading the gospel message everywhere. It is what Jesus expects us to do.

Paul at Athens

"Now while Paul waited for them at Athens, his spirit was provoked within him when he saw that the city was given over to idols. Therefore, he reasoned in the synagogue with the Jews and with the Gentile worshipers, and in the marketplace daily with those who happened to be there. Then certain Epicurean and Stoic philosophers encountered him. And some said, 'What does this babbler want to say?'

Others said, 'He seems to be a proclaimer of foreign gods,' because he preached to them Jesus and the resurrection.

And they took him and brought him to the Areopagus, saying, 'May we know what this new doctrine is of which you speak? For you are bringing some strange things to our ears. Therefore, we want to know what these things mean.' For all the Athenians and the foreigners who were there spent their time in nothing else but either to tell or to hear some new thing.

Then Paul stood in the midst of the Areopagus and said, 'Men of Athens, I perceive that in all things you are very religious; for as I was passing through and considering the objects of your worship, I even found an altar with this inscription:

TO THE UNKNOWN GOD

Therefore, the One whom you worship without knowing, Him I proclaim to you: God, who made the world and everything in it, since He is Lord of heaven and earth, does not dwell in temples made with hands. Nor is He worshiped with men's hands, as though He needed anything, since He gives to all life, breath, and all things. And He has made from one blood every nation of men to dwell on all the face of the earth, and has determined their pre-appointed times and the boundaries of their dwellings, so that they should seek the Lord, in the hope that they might grope for Him and find Him, though He is not far from each one of us; for in Him we live and move and have our being, as also some of your own poets have said, "For we are also His offspring." Therefore, since we are the offspring of God, we ought not to think that the Divine Nature is like gold or silver or stone, something shaped by art and man's devising. Truly, these times of ignorance God overlooked, but now commands all men everywhere to repent, because He has appointed a day on which He will judge the world in righteousness by the Man whom He has ordained. He has given assurance of this to all by raising Him from the dead.'

And when they heard of the resurrection of the dead, some mocked, while others said, 'We will hear you again on this matter.' So, Paul departed from among them. However, some men joined him and believed, among them Dionysius the Areopagite, a woman named Damaris, and others with them." Acts 17:16-34

J. W. McGarvey (Acts of the Apostles, pp. 118-120) gives some interesting facts about the culture of Athens and the philosophies mentioned here. The Greeks had developed "the most profound philosophy, the most glowing eloquence, the most exquisite poetry. And the most refined creative art which the world has ever seen." But their society had become completely corrupt and abandoned "to every vice which passion could prompt or imagination could invent." (p. 118) He points out the catalogue of those vices given by Paul in Romans 1:26-32. Speaking of the depths to which mankind had fallen, he says:

"For this reason, God gave them up to vile passions. For even their women exchanged the natural use for what is against nature. Likewise, also the men, leaving the natural use of the woman, burned in their lust for one another, men with men committing what is shameful, and receiving in themselves the penalty of their error which was due.

And even as they did not like to retain God in their knowledge, God gave them over to a debased mind, to do those things which are not fitting; being filled with all unrighteousness, sexual immorality, wickedness, covetousness, maliciousness; full of envy, murder, strife, deceit, evil-mindedness; they are whisperers, backbiters, haters of God, violent, proud, boasters, inventors of evil things, disobedient to parents, undiscerning, untrustworthy, unloving, unforgiving, unmerciful; who, knowing the righteous judgment of God, that those who practice such things are deserving of death, not only do the same but also approve of those who practice them."

McGarvey gives a brief description of the Epicurean and Stoic philosophies: "The Stoics taught that the greatest good in life was to be attained through a total indifference to both the sorrows and the pleasures of the world; the Epicureans, that it was to be obtained through the prudent gratification of every passion." (p. 120)

The stark contrast of the teachings of Jesus to these human philosophies is obvious. He teaches us to love our neighbors as ourselves, to reject all ungodliness and worldly lusts, and to keep ourselves unspotted from the world.

The Areopagus was a location in Athens where the leaders and philosophers met to engage in discussions. It seemed appropriate to the men of Athens to take Paul there and have him explain these new ideas about what they called "foreign gods."

His address to them is, or began to be, a wonderful explanation of the truth about Jesus. He began where they were.

"Men of Athens, I perceive that in all things you are very religious; for as I was passing through and considering the objects of your worship, I even found this inscription:

TO THE UNKNOWN GOD.

Therefore, the One whom you worship without knowing, Him I proclaim to you." Acts 17:22-23

It was the perfect place to start with people who did not know the One true God. Although there were Jews in cities all over the Roman empire, the average Athenian probably knew next to nothing about the God of the Jews.

The Greek gods were somewhat like superhumans who had great powers but also had all the faults and vices of humans. They were to be feared for their power and their tempers, admired for their beauty, but certainly not loved.

Paul taught the Athenians that the One true God is the Creator. They had no such concept of God. All of their gods would naturally be inferior to such a One. He taught that God does not dwell in manmade temples, that He does not need anything we can give Him, such as food and drink and shelter. Instead, He gives us life and all we have. These were things they did not attribute to their gods. These ideas about God were far superior to anything they believed.

He taught them that all human beings are descendants of one ancestor created by God. He taught that the God of Heaven controls all things. He determines when nations rise and fall. He decides where they reside and what territory they control. They believed each nation had its own deity, that territory belonged to a god, and he gave control of it to his people. The idea of one all powerful God was new to them.

Paul taught that we are God's offspring, so we should not think the nature of God is like gold or silver or stone shaped by man's art and imagination. He also told them that God has, in past times, overlooked man's ignorance, but He now commands all men everywhere to repent. They must not think of him in the old ways, but as He truly is, because a judgment day is coming. He will judge the world in righteousness by the Man He has ordained. He has given assurance of this to all people by raising Him from the dead. God set the seal of approval on the life of Christ and made Him the standard by which He will judge all people.

They listened to Paul until he mentioned the resurrection, then some began to mock him, but others wanted to hear more about it. There were some who joined Paul and Silas, which I assume means they believed and were baptized.

The words of Paul are meant for us as well as for the Athenians. He is certainly our Savior, but He is also our Judge. One day, He is coming to judge the world in righteousness. We must answer one question. Are we ready?

Discussion Questions
Chapter 15

1. Why do you think Paul always seemed to stir up the enemies of the faith?

2. Why were the enemies of Christ so violently opposed to the church?

3. Why don't people rise against us when we preach the truth? Do you think they would become violent if we preached strongly against abortion, pornography, and drinking?

4. Why do you think people in high positions in the political world are seldom devout followers of Christ?

5. Is the influence of the world creeping into the church? How?

Chapter 16

Paul at Corinth

"After these things Paul departed from Athens and went to Corinth. And he found a certain Jew named Aquila, born in Pontus, who had recently come from Italy with his wife Priscilla (because Claudius had commanded all the Jews to depart from Rome); and he came to them. So, because he was of the same trade, he stayed with them and worked; for by occupation they were tentmakers. And he reasoned in the synagogue every Sabbath, and persuaded both Jews and Greeks." **Acts 18:1-4**

The story of Paul at Corinth shows that even the strongest of Christians can have periods of depression and underproductivity. He came there after a rather bad time in Athens. The intellectuals in the Greek capital had, for the most part, scoffed at his testimony about Jesus. Relatively speaking, he had failed there. When he left there and made his way to Corinth, he was alone. He had no companions to encourage him. In describing the time later, he said to the Corinthians. "And I, brethren, when I came to you, did not come with excellence of speech or of wisdom declaring to you the testimony of God. For I determined not to know anything among you except Jesus Christ and Him crucified. I was with you in weakness, in fear, and in much trembling" (1 Corinthians 2:1-3).

The first seventeen verses of Acts 18 divide naturally into three sections: the beginning, verses 1-8, the vision, verses 9-11, and the Gallio incident, verses 12-17.

The first phase of Paul's work in Corinth began when he took a job making tents. He had arrived in this great commercial center of the area with no resources to sustain him, so it became necessary to take a job to meet his need for food and lodging. By the grace of God, he found both a man named Aquila and his wife, Priscilla. They apparently were in the business of tent making and were able to hire Paul and provide a place for him to stay. We are not told if they were already Christians or if they were led to Christ by Paul, but we know from other references to them in the New Testament that they were co-workers with Paul in the church. (Romans 16:19,1 Corinthians 16:19)

Paul's preaching in the synagogue did not at first stir up trouble, but after Silas and Timothy joined him, things began to happen. Luke seems to indicate that Paul's preaching changed. Previously, he had described preaching as reasoning and persuading both Jews and Greeks. After the arrival of his companions, Luke says Paul was compelled by the Spirit and testified that Jesus was the Christ. That's when the opposition stood up, opposed him, and blasphemed.

At that point, he left the synagogue. He shook his clothes and said, "Your blood be upon your own heads; I am clean. From now on I will go to the Gentiles" (Acts 18:6). He did not move far. A man named Justus lived next door to the synagogue. Paul made that his base of operation from that time forward. His ministry really began to become effective when many Corinthians became Christians, including Crispus, the ruler of the synagogue.

The second portion of this chapter begins in verse nine. It tells of a vision Paul had in which the Lord spoke to him, saying, "Do not be afraid, but speak, and do not keep silent; for I am with you, and no one will attack you to hurt you; for I have many people in this city" (Acts 18:9-10).

Corinth was the commercial hub of the area. There were direct trade routes by sea from Corinth to Ephesus and Asia to the East and to Rome and all the surrounding area to the west. When Paul was there, it had a population of about 90,000. The streets were paved with marble, and statues stood all along them. It was thriving financially, but it was a hotbed of vile and corrupt idol worship. It may well be that Paul was in desperate need of encouragement from the Lord. After the vision, he remained in Corinth for another eighteen months. It was the longest he had stayed at one place in his ministry up to that time.

The last section of chapter eighteen begins in verse twelve. The Jews who opposed Paul and the gospel acted against him. They arrested him and brought him before the proconsul whose name was Gallio. Archaeologists have found a coin that bears the image of Gallio, which was minted when he was in Corinth. Because of it, we know that he was the proconsul there in 51 and 52 A.D., and it allows us to develop an accurate chronology of Paul's ministry.

When the Jews brought Paul to his judgment seat, he threw out the case because it involved Jewish, not Roman law. He said, "I do not want to be a judge of such matters" (Acts 18:15). When he drove the Jews from the judgment seat, the Greeks beat Sosthenes, the ruler of the synagogue before the judgment seat, and Gallio did not take notice of their actions.

As a side note, if you go to Greece and visit the site of ancient Corinth, you will be able to see the site of the judgment seat. The proconsul was seated on an elevated platform from which he could look down on the litigators. Diane and I went there on a trip to celebrate our fiftieth wedding anniversary.

Although worldly judges generally feel the same way Gallio did about judging in matters concerning the gospel, brushing them off as of little importance, the truth is that there are no more important matters, for they deal with our eternal life.

It may be that Sosthenes, the ruler of the synagogue, learned from this experience. Years later, when Paul wrote to the Corinthians, he sent greetings from himself and "Sosthenes our brother" (1 Corinthians 1:1). We don't know if it is the same Sosthenes, but it seems likely it is.

This is another incident that illustrates how the joy Christians have in the Lord enables them to rise above trying circumstances.

From Antioch to Ephesus

"So Paul still remained a good while. Then he took leave of the brethren and sailed for Syria, and Priscilla and Aquila were with him. He had his hair cut off at Cenchrea, for he had taken a vow. And he came to Ephesus, and left them there; but he himself entered the synagogue and reasoned with the Jews. When they asked him to stay a longer time with them, he did not consent, but took leave of them, saying, 'I must by all means keep this coming feast in Jerusalem; but I will return again to you, God willing.' And he sailed from Ephesus.

And when he had landed at Caesarea, and gone up and greeted the church, he went down to Antioch. After he had spent some time there, he departed and went over the region of Galatia and Phrygia in order, strengthening all the disciples." Acts 18:18-23

This portion of Acts 18 might well have been included in chapter nineteen because it places Paul at Ephesus, where the next significant action takes place. It begins with him leaving Corinth, and he traveled as far as

Ephesus with Priscilla and Aquila. I find it interesting that Luke begins at this point to refer to this couple using the woman's name first. He had previously called them Aquila and Priscilla. It probably means that she was the stronger of the two personalities and took the lead in their work.

Paul went to the synagogue there and began reasoning with them, but he refused to stay longer because he was determined to keep the upcoming feast in Jerusalem. He told them he would return and kept that promise not long afterwards.

After he left, an eloquent man named Apollos came to Ephesus and began teaching in the synagogue. Although he knew about Jesus, he only was instructed in the baptism of John. Aquila and Priscilla took him aside and explained about Christian baptism. Luke puts Aquila first here because he took the lead in teaching Apollos. After they taught him, he left to go to Achaia and encourage and strengthen the disciples there.

Paul at Ephesus

"And it happened, while Apollos was at Corinth, that Paul, having passed through the upper regions, came to Ephesus." Acts 19:1

When Paul returned to Ephesus, he found some disciples there. Having seen no evidence of the presence of supernatural gifts of the Holy Spirit, he asked them if they had received the Holy Spirit. Their answer led him to ask a second question. Because they were unaware of the teachings concerning the Holy Spirit, it was the logical conclusion that they had not received Christian baptism. When he learned they had only received the baptism taught by John the Baptist, he proceeded to baptize them into the name of the Father, and of the Son, and of the Holy Spirit. Following their baptism, he laid his hands on them; and the Holy Spirit came upon them so that they were able to speak in foreign languages and prophesy.

This was the beginning of Paul's work in Ephesus. He labored for a while in the synagogue, teaching them about Jesus and the kingdom of God. As it always happened, the unbelievers rose up against him and spoke evil against the Way of Christ. At that point, Paul withdrew with the disciples and began teaching daily in the school of a man named Tyrannus. This continued for two years. The word spread during that time so that all of ancient Asia heard the gospel. When we read of the seven churches of Asia in Revelation, they are the ones that were started at this time.

God blessed Paul's ministry there with a period of miracles such as had not been seen since the early days of the church in Jerusalem, when they brought people out into the streets so that the shadow of Peter might fall on them (Acts 5:15-16), and a multitude were healed. In this case, in Ephesus, they brought handkerchiefs or aprons from him to the sick, and they were healed, and demons went out of many.

Two unusual things happened at this time. Some unbelieving Jews attempted to cast out demons, invoking the name of "Jesus whom Paul preaches." The evil spirit answered, "Jesus I know, and Paul I know; but who are you?" Then the man with the evil spirit attacked them and drove them out of the house naked and wounded.

Following that episode, many who had practiced magic in the city were converted; and they brought their books together and burned them. The value of the books was about fifty thousand pieces of silver. McGarvey (p. 157) says that the pieces of silver were "Attic di-drachmas," which were approximately equal to the Roman denarius in value. We know that the denarius was the amount commonly paid to a laborer for a day of work. It was an enormous sum. There must have been a multitude of those who practiced magic.

It was after this that trouble arose in Ephesus over the ministry of Paul and the Christians. We will take a look at what happened in a moment, but let me say that the normal sequence of events in a ministry that is bringing people to Christ is that when a period of growth occurs, Satan stirs up trouble. It may arise from within the church or come from outside. It can take many forms. I was serving a small church in a southern state. When we moved there, the average attendance on a Sunday morning was about 100. During our first year there, we added forty new members. There was great excitement in the church. Attendance on Sunday morning increased nearly forty percent, and we began having 100 people come back for Sunday evening services and about eighty for Wednesday night. That was a significant increase for both. I know all this doesn't sound that great to many of you, but to compare, the First Christian Church in Carthage, Missouri, which I served later, had a Sunday morning attendance of nearly 500. A similar percentage of increase for that church in one year would have meant nearly 200 people added in one year. To get back to the point I was making, that little church was attacked by Satan. He stirred up one church member to mount a campaign against me. He was determined to get rid of me. I never understood why, but he succeeded in wreaking havoc in the church. Now, many years later, that church no longer exists.

In Ephesus, a silversmith named Demetrius caused trouble for the Christians. He and his fellow craftsmen had developed a lucrative business by making silver shrines for people to use in their homes in the worship of Diana of the Ephesians.

If you go to the ruins of Ephesus today, you can see where the temple of Diana stood and visit the ruins of the outdoor theater, which are still in great shape. If you ever have a chance to visit the ruins of Ephesus, you will be impressed by the beauty of what remains there. They will show you a shop which they claim was Paul's tent making business. It cannot be proved, but is an interesting part of the ancient city.

The temple was one of the seven wonders of the ancient world. It was four hundred twenty-five feet long and one hundred twenty feet wide. It had one hundred twenty marble columns, which stood sixty-five feet high. They were erected along the four sides of the temple and were less than four feet apart. (McGarvey) The image of Diana was a crude figure of a many breasted woman, a symbol of the ability to produce abundant offspring.

The impact of Paul's ministry in Ephesus was such that the silversmiths were concerned about losing business because so many were turning away from idol worship to the One true God and Jesus Christ. Christianity was having a major impact on the city. Demetrius started a riot by calling out the worshippers of Diana in opposition to the Christians. The story is remarkable in how the riot ended. The crowds shouting, "Great is Diana of the Ephesians," rushed into the theater, having seized two of Paul's travel companions. Many in the crowd didn't even know what the commotion was all about. The riot ended when a wise city clerk quieted the crowd and addressed them briefly, pointing out that the courts were open as the proper place to address their concerns. He then warned them of the possibility of the Romans calling them to account for their disorderly gathering. He had been successful in getting the crowd to calm down, and his warning about the Romans seemed to make them think better of their actions. They acquiesced when he dismissed the assembly.

At that point, Paul apparently thought it would be best for the Christians in Ephesus if he left. He called the disciples together, embraced them, and departed for Macedonia. Evidently, it diffused the situation so that there was no other trouble for the church at Ephesus at that time.

Paul and his companions labored for a while in Macedonia, encouraging the Christians, and then moved on to Greece. He stayed there for three months and departed when the Jews plotted against him. His party left from Philippi and made their way to Troas.

Troas and Beyond

"After the uproar had ceased, Paul called the disciples to himself, embraced them, and departed to go to Macedonia. Now when he had gone over that region and encouraged them with many words, he came to Greece and stayed three months. And when the Jews plotted against him as he was about to sail to Syria, he decided to return through Macedonia. And Sopater of Berea accompanied him to Asia—also Aristarchus and Secundus of the Thessalonians, and Gaius of Derbe, and Timothy, and Tychicus and Trophimus of Asia. These men, going ahead, waited for us at Troas. But we sailed away from Philippi after the Days of Unleavened Bread, and in five days joined them at Troas, where we stayed seven days." Acts 20:1-7

Paul's ministry at Troas was brief, but it is instructive concerning the worship services in New Testament times. First, the ordinary meeting of the church occurred on the first day of the week. Paul was ready to speak to them when they met. The fact that he continued speaking until midnight suggests that they met in the evening. It does not mention any break for meals, so it seems likely that they did not meet early in the day. After dark on the seventh day, they would have called it the first day of the week, so they probably met on Saturday night. We don't know this for certain, but it is likely. The observance of the Lord's Supper would have been on the first day of the week, whether it was Saturday night or Sunday morning.

The story of Eutychus is another illustration of the compassion of the Lord and His people. From what we have studied in Acts, we understand that the Holy Spirit prompted healings; therefore, this was the Lord's decision to raise Eutychus from the dead. The last statement of this story is typically understated. The Bible rarely comments on the emotional response to an occurrence. To say they were "not a little comforted" is rather subdued. The grief they would have experienced if he had not been raised would have been excruciating.

Verse seven of chapter twenty clearly states that they met to break bread, that is, to observe the Lord's Supper. This verse gives us the example we use to justify our practice of meeting on the first day of every week to have the Lord's Supper. It is the focal point of our worship service. We focus our minds on Jesus and the sacrifice He made on our behalf.

When Paul and his company left Troas, the others went by ship. The next port of call was Assos, a distance of about forty miles by ship. Paul directed them to go on without him since he intended to walk across the peninsula to Assos. On foot, the trip would have been about twenty miles. He may have been able to make the entire trip that day since they were accustomed to walking long distances in a day. It would have been a difficult trip for him since they had been up the whole night, but he may have been unable to rest because of the tremendous excitement and stress of the past day. At any rate, he probably was at Assos when the ship arrived, and they took him on board for the rest of the journey to Miletus.

Paul and the Elders from Ephesus

"From Miletus he sent to Ephesus and called for the elders of the church. And when they had come to him, he said to them: 'You know, from the first day that I came to Asia, in what manner I always lived among you, serving the Lord with all humility, with many tears and trials which happened to me by the plotting of the Jews; how I kept back nothing that was helpful, but proclaimed it to you, and taught you publicly and from house to house, testifying to Jews, and also to Greeks, repentance toward God and faith toward our Lord Jesus Christ. And see, now I go bound in the spirit to Jerusalem, not knowing the things that will happen to me there, except that the Holy Spirit testifies in every city, saying that chains and tribulations await me. But none of these things move me; nor do I count my life dear to myself, so that I may finish my race with joy, and the ministry which I received from the Lord Jesus, to testify to the gospel of the grace of God.

And indeed, now I know that you all, among whom I have gone preaching the kingdom of God, will see my face no more. Therefore, I testify to you this day that I am innocent of the blood of all men. For I have not shunned to declare to you the whole counsel of God. Therefore, take heed to yourselves and to all the flock, among which the Holy Spirit has made you overseers, to shepherd the church of God which He purchased with His own blood.'" Acts 20:17-28

This passage is very instructive concerning the leadership of the local churches in the New Testament. The men Paul summoned to Miletus in verse seventeen are called Elders. In verse twenty-eight, he says the Holy Spirit had made them overseers and that they should shepherd the church.

The word translated elder is used often in Acts to speak of leaders in the churches. When Paul and Barnabas went to Jerusalem to discuss the question of the Gentiles and the law of Moses, they met with the apostles and elders (Acts 15:2,6). In chapter 14, verse 23, we see that they appointed elders in every church. The word translated overseers is translated bishops in Philippians 1:1, and in 1 Timothy 3:2 and Titus 1:7. This leads us to the conclusion that these two words or titles were given to the same leaders of the church. They were used interchangeably.

Again, we learn from verse twenty-eight that their job included shepherding and overseeing the flock or church. If we follow the example of the New Testament, we will choose qualified men in the church to serve in the position of elder and to do the work of overseer and shepherd.

In practice in the twenty-first century church in America, we go through the motions of appointing elders in every church, but they seldom do the job of shepherding the flock. They make decisions as overseers, but do not shepherd the flock, and often do not meet the qualifications for the position spelled out for us in 1 Timothy and Titus. The apostle Paul warned Timothy of the danger of hasty selection of men to be elders in 1 Timothy 5:22, "Do not lay hands on anyone hastily, nor share in other people's sins; keep yourself pure." The laying on of hands refers to the ritual of setting men apart for the position of elder.

If we look at verses 20 through 21 of this passage, we will see Paul's description of the work he did among them. He says, "I kept back nothing that was helpful, but proclaimed it to you, and taught you publicly and from house to house, testifying to Jews, and also to Greeks, repentance toward God and faith toward our Lord Jesus Christ." This is the example for those of us who serve as evangelists in the church. The elders are to be shepherds who care for the needs of the flock and teachers, as well as overseers.

In verses 29-32, Paul admonishes the elders with these words:

"For I know this, that after my departure savage wolves will come in among you, not sparing the flock. Also, from among yourselves men will rise, speaking perverse things, to draw away the disciples after themselves. Therefore, watch, and remember that for three years I did not cease to warn everyone night and day with tears.

So now, brethren, I commend you to God and to the word of His grace, which can build you up and give you an inheritance among all those who are sanctified."

If the elders will do the job of shepherds and overseers, preachers can do the job of evangelists, and the church can fulfill the mission given to us by our Savior.

Having commended the elders to God and told them they would never see him again, he knelt with them and prayed. They wept freely because they would see him no more; then they accompanied him to the ship that would take him away.

Discussion Questions

Chapter 16

1. Do you think it was the encouragement of Silas and Timothy that led Paul to speak more boldly in the Synagogues about Christ?

2. Why did Paul work at tentmaking while he was in Corinth? Do you think he did that in other places?

3. Do you think the example of the church in Troas, in observing the Lord's Supper every week is one we should follow? Why or why not?

4. When Paul addressed the elders of Ephesus, he said God had made them overseers and admonished them to feed the flock. Did their job include exercising oversight and shepherding? Do we expect our Elders to be shepherds? Do they take that responsibility seriously? Do they expect the preacher to be the shepherd?

Chapter 17

Arrested in Jerusalem

"Then Paul took the men, and the next day, having been purified with them, entered the temple to announce the expiration of the days of purification, at which time an offering should be made for each one of them.

Now when the seven days were almost ended, the Jews from Asia, seeing him in the temple, stirred up the whole crowd and laid hands on him, crying out, 'Men of Israel, help! This is the man who teaches all men everywhere against the people, the law, and this place; and furthermore he also brought Greeks into the temple and has defiled this holy place.' (For they had previously seen Trophimus the Ephesian with him in the city, whom they supposed that Paul had brought into the temple.)

And all the city was disturbed; and the people ran together, seized Paul, and dragged him out of the temple; and immediately the doors were shut. Now as they were seeking to kill him, news came to the commander of the garrison that all Jerusalem was in an uproar. He immediately took soldiers and centurions, and ran down to them. And when they saw the commander and the soldiers, they stopped beating Paul. Then the commander came near and took him, and commanded him to be bound with two chains; and he asked who he was and what he had done. And some among the multitude cried one thing and some another.

So when he could not ascertain the truth because of the tumult, he commanded him to be taken into the barracks. When he reached the stairs, he had to be carried by the soldiers because of the violence of the mob. For the multitude of the people followed after, crying out, 'Away with him!'"

Acts 21:28-36

The voyage from Miletus to Phoenicia was uneventful. When they landed at Tyre, the ship unloaded its cargo. Paul and his companions disembarked and remained in Tyre for seven days. At that time, the disciples told him by the Spirit not to go to Jerusalem, but the Lord was directing him to go there. He was carrying with him a large sum of money, which had been contributed by the Gentile churches for the suffering saints in Judea. (See 2 Corinthians 9:1-15.)

From Tyre, they made their way on board a ship which took them to Ptolemais, where they greeted the disciple and stayed one day. The next day, they made their way to Caesarea, where they stayed for many days in the home of Philip the evangelist, who was one of the first seven deacons appointed by the church in Jerusalem. He had apparently settled there in Caesarea and continued teaching and evangelizing in the area.

Verse nine tells us that he had four virgin daughters who prophesied. That is to say, they had the gift of prophecy. Since we know the gift was given through the laying on of an apostle's hands, it means that at some time the Holy Spirit had directed an apostle to bestow that gift upon them. The question then arises, "To whom did they prophesy?" Paul wrote to the Corinthians, "Let your women keep silent in the churches, for they are not permitted to speak; but they are to be submissive, as the law also says. And if they want to learn something, let them ask their own husbands at home; for it is shameful for women to speak in church." He also wrote to Timothy, "Let a woman learn in silence with all submission. And I do not permit a woman to teach or to have authority over a man, but to be in silence" (1 Timothy 2:11-12). Were they only allowed to prophesy to other women or children? The fact that both Aquila and Priscilla were involved in the teaching of Apollos (Acts 18:26) would seem to indicate that women were allowed to teach men privately or as partners with their husbands.

There is more that could be said about this subject, but this is not the best time to discuss it extensively.

McGarvey (Acts of the Apostles, Introduction pp. XXVI–XXXIV) has an extensive discussion of the chronology of this book. He places the conversion of Saul in 36 A.D. at about the same time Philip began his work in Caesarea, Paul's work with Barnabas beginning in Antioch in 43 A.D., his three missionary tours from 44-58, with his time with Philip in Caesarea early in 58. After Philip baptized the Ethiopian (Acts 8:26-40), "he was found at Azotus. And passing through, he preached in all the cities till he came to Caesarea." This means that Philip had been living and preaching in that area for about twenty-two years. In that time, he had become rather prosperous since he was able to provide a place to stay for Paul and his eight companions.

After they had been there many days with Philip, a prophet named Agabus came down from Judea. He took Paul's belt, bound his own hands and feet, and said, "Thus says the Holy Spirit, 'So shall the Jews at Jerusalem bind the man who owns this belt, and deliver him into the hands of the Gentiles'" (Acts 21:11).

When Paul's companions and the Christians from Caesarea heard this prophecy, they begged him not to go to Jerusalem. He answered, "What do you mean by weeping and breaking my heart? For I am ready not only to be bound, but also to die at Jerusalem for the name of the Lord Jesus" (Acts 21:13). When they heard that they stopped pleading with him and said, "The will of the Lord be done" (verse 14).

Sometime later, they went to Jerusalem, accompanied by some disciples from Caesarea, including a man named Mnason of Cyprus, who had a house in Jerusalem where they were to stay. They were received gladly by the brethren in Jerusalem, but some of them had been told that Paul was teaching Jews who lived among the Gentiles to forsake the Law of Moses. They suggested that he join four men who had taken a vow, be purified with them, and pay their expenses to show the Jewish Christians that the rumors were not true.

At least two things are indicated by these verses. First, the Jewish Christians still thought it was proper for them to continue following the Law and the traditions of the elders. They did not discontinue these practices in the earliest days of the church. The circumstances were forever changed when the Romans destroyed the temple in 70 A.D. Second, Paul lived by the truth that there are things we are at liberty to do for the sake of others, and others that we must do to be obedient to God (McGarvey, p. 207). He did not, personally feel the need to continue these practices of the Jewish Law and tradition, but he did not find fault with those who did observe them, but only with those who would have made them mandatory.

It was in the observance of the requirements of the vow with the four men of Israel that Paul was seized, beaten, falsely accused, and then taken into custody by the Romans. The only identification of his accusers is that they were Jews from Asia. They must have recognized him as the man who escaped their plots against him in Ephesus. The accusation that he had brought Greeks into the temple was entirely false and seems to have been invented by them because of their hatred of him and his message (Acts 20:19).

Having stirred up the crowd by shouting that he had brought Greeks into the temple, they seized him and dragged him out of the court of Israel into the court of the Gentiles. The outer court of the temple, which included several acres of open space, was called the Court of Gentiles because foreigners were allowed there. They were barred from the inner courts; and warnings were inscribed beside the entrances informing them that entering there would be punishable by death.

The court of Gentiles was the only place in ancient Jerusalem where huge crowds could gather. The tower of Antonia stood on the northwestern angle of the court and had a flight of stone steps that led down from it into the court. The Roman garrison was quartered there. When a large group of soldiers showed up, the crowd released Paul into their custody. When Luke says that the commander of the garrison took soldiers and centurions down, the use of the plural in regard to centurions indicates there were hundreds of soldiers. A smaller group would have posed little threat to the mob and probably would not have saved Paul.

When the commander sought to determine who Paul was and what he had done, the confused responses of the mob led him to command his soldiers to take him into the barracks. It became necessary for them to pick up Paul and rush him up the stairs to escape the violence of the mob. As they were about to enter the barracks, Paul spoke to the commander in Greek. When he explained that he was a Jew from Tarsus and asked to be given permission to speak to the people, the commander was surprised that he spoke in the Greek language and granted his request.

When Paul began to speak to the crowd in Hebrew, it probably surprised the commander again. The common language spoken in Israel at the time was Aramaic. Now it is clear that Paul spoke at least three languages. He was obviously an educated man. Scholars believe that both Hebrew and Aramaic were spoken commonly in Israel at the time, with Aramaic beginning to predominate along about this time or a little later. The crowd in the temple was accustomed to hearing Hebrew spoken ordinarily by the Rabbis in their religious messages. Their recognition of the language of their religious heritage may have contributed to their willingness to hear what Paul was saying. There is no indication whether the commander spoke all three languages. He may not have understood fully what Paul said to the people.

When the apostle began to speak in Hebrew, the crowd grew quiet as they listened to his defense. His speech took them from his birth in Tarsus through his education in Jerusalem at the feet of the famous Rabbi Gamaliel, his early persecution of Christians, his encounter with Jesus of Nazareth on the road to Damascus, his baptism to wash away his sins, his return to Jerusalem, and his vision while praying in the temple when Jesus told him to leave Jerusalem. At that point, he noted that he had been a leader of the persecution and had actually been among those who approved when Stephen was stoned. But when he spoke of the words of the Lord which directed him to go far away to the Gentiles, they erupted with shouts calling for his execution.

At that time, the commander still had no idea what the commotion was all about, so he commanded that Paul should be examined under scourging. As they were binding him for the scourging, Paul asked the centurion in charge if it was lawful for him to beat a Roman who was not condemned. Then the centurion informed the commander that Paul was a Roman citizen. He then asked Paul if it was true. When Paul answered in the affirmative, the commander revealed that he had paid a large sum of money to acquire his citizenship. Paul responded that he was a citizen by birth. At that point, they became much more careful in their treatment of the apostle. It was as they were binding him in the process of preparing for the scourging that Paul spoke up, and the fact that they came that close to scourging a Roman citizen alarmed the commander.

Paul Sent to Felix

"The next day, because he wanted to know for certain why he was accused by the Jews, he released him from his bonds, and commanded the chief priests and all their council to appear, and brought Paul down and set him before them.

Then Paul, looking earnestly at the council, said, 'Men and brethren, I have lived in all good conscience before God until this day.' And the high priest Ananias commanded those who stood by him to strike him on the mouth. Then Paul said to him, 'God will strike you, you whitewashed wall! For you sit to judge me according to the law, and do you command me to be struck contrary to the law?'

And those who stood by said, 'Do you revile God's high priest?'

Then Paul said, 'I did not know, brethren, that he was the high priest; for it is written, 'You shall not speak evil of a ruler of your people.'

But when Paul perceived that one part were Sadducees and the other Pharisees, he cried out in the council, 'Men and brethren, I am a Pharisee, the son of a Pharisee; concerning the hope and resurrection of the dead I am being judged!'

And when he had said this, a dissension arose between the Pharisees and the Sadducees; and the assembly was divided." Acts 22:30-23:7

The Roman commander of the troops in Jerusalem was at a loss to know what charge was being brought against Paul, so he brought him before the council of the Jews to find out what it was. Paul began his defense by stating that everything he did was done with a clear conscience. The High Priest was angered by that statement and commanded that he be struck on the mouth. Paul's reply was classic. He called the High Priest a whitewashed wall and said God would strike him. When he was rebuked for speaking reviling words against the high priest, he said he did not realize the man was the high priest. Some have argued that Paul's thorn in the flesh must have been very poor eyesight because he should have recognized the clothing of the high priest. They also cite these words of Paul from Galatians 4:13-15

"You know that because of physical infirmity I preached the gospel to you at the first. And my trial, which was in my flesh, you did not despise or reject, but you received me as an angel of God, even as Christ Jesus. What then was the blessing you enjoyed? For I bear you witness that, if possible, you would have plucked out your own eyes and given them to me."

I am not sure that is correct, but it is certainly a possibility. They had no way of dealing with poor eyesight then, and there is no record of a servant of God ever using the powers given to him by God to heal himself.

Getting back to Paul's appearance before the Sanhedrin council, the apostle realized there were powerful men on the council who were Sadducees as well as many who were Pharisees. Seeing an opportunity to deadlock the council, he declared that he was a Pharisee and was being judged because of his hope in the resurrection from the dead. It had the desired effect. The commotion he aroused was so heated that the commander was afraid they would pull Paul apart, so he rescued Paul for a second time.

That night, the Lord appeared to Paul to comfort him with the statement that he would also bear witness for Him at Rome. The enemies of Paul were planning to ambush him and murder him before another day passed. They asked the chief priests and elders to have Paul brought before them again the next day to give them an opportunity to carry out their plan.

When Paul's nephew heard about the plot, he told his uncle, and Paul sent him to the commander with the information. When the young man told him about the plot, the commander took immediate action to protect his prisoner. He called two centurions and instructed them to prepare a formidable force to take Paul to the governor in the middle of the night. They gathered 200 soldiers, 70 horsemen, and 200 spearmen for the task. They left Jerusalem at about three or four o'clock in the morning. They took Paul about halfway to Caesarea that night. The next day, they sent the foot soldiers back and continued on horseback the rest of the way.

The commander sent a letter to Governor Felix explaining that he had rescued Paul from the Jews, having learned that he was a Roman. Which was not true, but it made him look better. He had no idea Paul was Roman at the time he took him into custody. He explained that the charges against him had to do with Jewish law, and there was nothing in the charges that made him deserving of death or imprisonment. He explained that he was sending the prisoner to him to save him from a plot of the Jews. When Felix learned Paul was from Cilicia, he said he would hear the case when his accusers came.

After five days, the high priest came with the elders and an orator named Tertullus to present the charges against Paul. The charges were as follows:

1. He was a troublemaker and creator of dissension among the Jews throughout the world.
2. He was a ringleader of the sect of the Nazarene, and
3. He tried to profane the temple.

The Jews who had come along agreed, maintaining that the charges were true.

When Paul was allowed to answer, he refuted each of the charges. First, he had only been in Jerusalem for twelve days, and they had not found him in the temple or synagogues disputing with anyone or inciting the crowd. Second, he worshipped God according to the way they called a sect. Third, he had brought alms to his nation and was in the temple purified with neither a mob nor tumult. When Felix had heard these arguments, it was obvious that Paul was not guilty of any punishable offense, but he postponed any decision on the charges and kept Paul in custody, treating him kindly. He allowed Paul's friends to visit him and provide for his needs. We learn later (v. 26) that he was hoping Paul's friends would bribe him to secure his release. Because the apostle would not be associated with bribery, he would not allow that to happen.

Felix was interested in learning more about the faith, so he sent for Paul and allowed him to speak to him and his wife, Drusilla. Commentators have given ample proof of the extreme cruelty and corruption of Felix from historians who wrote during that time. He rose from a slave to a ruler because of his relationship with the powerful woman who promoted him. Drusilla was the wife of another man, but was enticed to live with Felix in an adulterous relationship.

Paul was probably aware of the vile and evil life of the man, so when allowed to speak to the governor and his mistress, he reasoned about righteousness, self-control, and the judgment to come. The message struck fear into the heart of Felix, but not enough to convince him to turn from his wicked ways. He sent Paul away, saying that when he had a more convenient season, he would send for him. Of course, it was never convenient for him to change. Two years later, he was removed from his position and sent into exile with Drusilla. But because he wanted to do the Jews a favor, he kept Paul in custody to be dealt with by Porcius Festus, the new governor.

Discussion Questions

Chapter 17

1. Why do you think the Jewish Christians continued the rituals of the Law when they were no longer necessary? Do we have any traditions that are not required by the Scriptures?

2. Would it be appropriate for us to go into a synagogue today and preach about Jesus? What if we could agree to let a rabbi come to speak to our church, and one of us could speak at their service?

3. Do you think the Jews who plotted to assassinate Paul would have attacked the Roman soldiers to get at Paul if they had a large enough force?

4. Why were the disciples unwilling to bribe Felix to secure the release of Paul? Is there ever a time when it would be proper to bribe a government official to get him to release a brother who was arrested for preaching the gospel? Why or why not?

5. If you were allowed to speak to a joint session of the U.S. Congress, would you speak about righteous living and judgment? Would that be appropriate?

Chapter 18

Festus and the Appeal to Caesar

"Now when Festus had come to the province, after three days he went up from Caesarea to Jerusalem. Then the high priest and the chief men of the Jews informed him against Paul; and they petitioned him, asking a favor against him, that he would summon him to Jerusalem, while they lay in ambush along the road to kill him. But Festus answered that Paul should be kept at Caesarea, and that he himself was going there shortly. 'Therefore,' he said, 'let those who have authority among you go down with me and accuse this man, to see if there is any fault in him.'

And when he had remained among them more than ten days, he went down to Caesarea. And the next day, sitting on the judgment seat, he commanded Paul to be brought. When he had come, the Jews who had come down from Jerusalem stood about and laid many serious complaints against Paul, which they could not prove." **Acts 25:1-7**

When Paul stated that he had done nothing against the law of the Jews, nor against the temple, nor against Caesar, Festus recognized they had no credible charges against him, but wanting to do the Jews a favor, he asked Paul, "Are you willing to go up to Jerusalem and there be judged before me concerning these things?" (v. 9) Realizing that the Jews wanted him transported to Jerusalem so they could ambush him along the way and kill him, Paul answered by appealing to Caesar (vv. 10-11). When Festus had consulted with the council, he answered, "You have appealed to Caesar? To Caesar you shall go!"

Roman law required the judge in any case of appeal to Caesar to immediately suspend the trial and send the accused to Rome. His accusers would then be required to travel to Rome to press their charges. Paul probably thought the Jews would not go so far since they knew their charges were baseless.

In the time between his appeal to Caesar and the arrangements to transport him to Rome, Paul was allowed to speak to Festus, as well as King Agrippa and Bernice, about the faith. The occasion was brought about by the visit of Agrippa and Bernice to Caesarea to congratulate Festus on his appointment as governor of the area. It was customary for rulers of neighboring provinces to extend such congratulations to those who had just been appointed. Agrippa was the son of Herod who had murdered James and arrested Peter. That particular Herod died when Agrippa was only seventeen years old. At this time, Agrippa was governor of a district east of the Jordan River.

Festus wanted Agrippa's greater knowledge concerning Jewish laws and customs to assist him concerning what he should write to Caesar about Paul. Agrippa said he would like to hear what Paul had to say, so Festus arranged for the apostle to speak before an assembly consisting of Agrippa, Bernice, prominent men of Caesarea, and himself. When Paul was brought in, Festus explained the situation to the audience, and Agrippa invited Paul to speak.

In his opening remarks, the apostle expressed pleasure at being allowed to present his defense before the king, seeing that he was an expert in customs and questions about the Jews. He did not mention that it gave him an opportunity to present the gospel message to an audience of powerful men of the world. He must have been excited about preaching to such an assembly.

He began his message by reciting his personal history from persecutor of the followers of Jesus to champion of their cause. He told of casting his vote against those who were executed. Then he told them of his encounter with Jesus on the way to Damascus. Everything in Paul's sermon was designed to convince his audience of the truth about Jesus. If he could have convinced the king that Jesus was the Messiah, it would have been a major step in making Christianity acceptable in Roman circles. But that would only be if Agrippa had been obedient to the faith. It is never convenient for a worldly man to become a Christian. There is too much (in his mind) to give up. It demands a change too radical for him to accept, even though it brings the promise of eternal life. Of course, we know that there is no other logical reaction if one truly believes Jesus is the Son of God who became a man to save us from our sins. We must bow down before Him, surrender our lives to Him to serve Him with all we have and all we are.

Paul explained that he preached that all people everywhere should repent, turn to God, and do works befitting repentance. The word translated repent means to change one's mind. Paul was saying that Agrippa and all in his audience should change their whole attitude toward life. Life has a purpose. They should change from an attitude that says, "Life is to be lived for pleasure," to one that says, "We should live for Him who died for us."

Festus reacted as the world often reacts to the gospel. He suddenly cried out. "Paul, you are beside yourself! Much learning is driving you mad!" The apostle responded by saying,

"I am not mad, most noble Festus, but speak the words of truth and reason. For the king, before whom I also speak freely, knows these things;

for I am convinced that none of these things escapes his attention, since this thing was not done in a corner. King Agrippa, do you believe the prophets? I know that you do believe." Acts 26:24-27

He made this appeal to Agrippa, directly confronting him and asking him to repent. Agrippa recognized what Paul intended, and responded, "Do you think that in such a short time you can persuade me to be a Christian?" (Acts 26:28 NIV) The NIV gives a more accurate translation of the king's response to Paul. It was not that Paul almost persuaded him to become a Christian, but that he was not going to be so easily convinced to change his whole way of living. It would have meant a truly radical change for him and would have brought the scorn of most of those who were in his circle. He was just not ready to make such a change.

Paul responded that he hoped that not just Agrippa, but all who heard him that day would become as he was, except for the chains that bound him. At that point, Agrippa stood up and effectively ended the proceedings. It was not until centuries later that a Roman monarch (Constantine) became a follower of Jesus.

Agrippa concluded that Paul might have been set free if he had not appealed to Caesar. When it became convenient for him to do so, Festus delivered Paul to a centurion named Julius to convey him and some other prisoners to Rome.

The Voyage to Rome

"And when it was decided that we should sail to Italy, they delivered Paul and some other prisoners to one named Julius, a centurion of the Augustan Regiment. So, entering a ship of Adramyttium, we put to sea, meaning to sail along the coasts of Asia. Aristarchus, a Macedonian of

Thessalonica, was with us." Acts 27:1-2

The first leg of their journey took them to Sidon. From there they sailed to the east of Cyprus, traveling north before they turned to the west and landed at Myra, a city in Lycia. There, they transferred to a ship headed for Italy. They set sail again and made their way with some difficulty to a harbor called Fair Havens on the island of Crete. It was not a port that was suitable for wintering in. "It might be an open road or bay, and having nothing to shelter from the boisterous waves, was a place very improper for a ship to be in, in stormy weather." (Gill's Exposition of the Entire Bible) They put to sea once more hoping to reach Phoenix so they could spend the winter there. Paul had advised them to remain where they were because their voyage would end in disaster, but they followed the advice of the helmsman and the owner of the ship and set sail. For a short time, they sailed west remaining close to Crete, but a storm arose which drove the ship for several days.

Paul's reason for advising them to remain at Fair Havens was that winter was approaching and sailing would become dangerous during that season. When it says the Fast was already over, it is referring to the only fast prescribed by the law of Moses, which was on the Day of Atonement, which usually occurs in our month of October. The storm that arose drove them for many days; and they did everything they knew to do to save the ship, but finally gave up all hope of surviving.

Everyone on board had fasted and prayed for delivery from the storm, until they were at the point of despair when Paul stood up in their midst and said,

"Men, you should have listened to me, and not have sailed from Crete and incurred this disaster and loss. And now I urge you to take heart, for there will be no loss of life among you, but only of the ship. For there stood by me this night an angel of the God to whom I belong and whom I serve, saying, 'Do not be afraid, Paul; you must be brought before Caesar; and indeed God has granted you all those who sail with you.' Therefore, take heart, men, for I believe God that it will be just as it was told me. However, we must run aground on a certain island." Acts 27:21-26

On the fourteenth night the sailors sensed that they were nearing land so they took soundings and determined that the water was becoming shallower. Fearing that they were about to run aground, they dropped four anchors from the stern of the ship and prayed for daylight to come. They have a museum on the island of Malta which has anchors retrieved from the sea nearby by which were the kind used at the time Paul and his companions were shipwrecked. It is another poof of the accuracy of the book of Acts. The sailors were planning to escape and save themselves, but Paul informed the centurion that they would all be lost if these men left the ship. So, the soldiers cut the skiff loose so that it fell into the sea.

When day was about to dawn, Paul urged them to eat saying, "Therefore I urge you to take nourishment, for this is for your survival, since not a hair will fall from the head of any of you" (Acts 27:34). Then he took some bread, gave thanks to God, and began to eat. All of the others on board (276 people) also began to eat. When they had all had enough, they threw the cargo of wheat into the sea.

When it was day, they cut the anchors loose and sought to run the ship up on a beach they sighted. They soon ran the ship aground so that the prow stuck fast and the stern began to break up. The soldiers intended to kill all the prisoners to prevent them from escaping, but the centurion stopped them because he wanted to save Paul. He commanded everyone who could swim to jump overboard first, then the rest clung to boards or parts of the ship and made it safely to land.

The people of the island called Malta, kindled a fire and welcomed them because it was raining and cold. Paul gathered some sticks to add to the fire, and a viper aroused by the heat came out of the bundle of sticks and fastened to his hand. The people of the island thought he was a murderer, thinking that even though he escaped the storm, justice would not allow him to live. But when he shook the creature off into the fire and suffered no ill effects, they changed their minds and said he was a god.

From Malta to Rome

"In that region there was an estate of the leading citizen of the island, whose name was Publius, who received us and entertained us courteously for three days. And it happened that the father of Publius lay sick of a fever and dysentery. Paul went in to him and prayed, and he laid his hands on him and healed him. So, when this was done, the rest of those on the island who had diseases also came and were healed. They also honored us in many ways; and when we departed, they provided such things as were necessary." Acts 28:7-10

The population of Malta in modern times is more than 100,000, but was likely only a fraction of that number when Paul was there. The beach where they found refuge is on the north-eastern end of the island, which is about seventeen miles long and nine miles wide. When the Lord used Paul to heal the father of the governor, the word quickly spread throughout the entire area. As a result, people came from everywhere to be healed. They were not disappointed, for God healed them all. Although Luke does not mention it, there is no doubt that Paul preached the gospel to them, and many believed and obeyed. The island may have been completely transformed in the three months they were there. When they departed to complete the journey to Rome, they were supplied with everything they needed for the trip. The generosity of the people of Malta was a response to the great good Paul had brought to the island by healing their sick.

They set sail for Italy in an Alexandrian ship, which was likely bringing a cargo of wheat from Egypt. The figure of the twin brothers, which stood most likely at the bow of the ship, was Castor and Pollux, the sons of Jupiter in their mythology, who were the supposed guardians of sailors. Their first stop was at Syracuse on the island of Sicily. After three days, they continued their journey with a stop at Rhegium, the southernmost port in Italy. Then a south wind sprang up, which allowed them to travel about 180 miles to Puteoli in a single day. There, they disembarked to travel the remaining 150 miles to Rome on foot.

The statement in Acts 28:13-14 is remarkable, "The next day we came to Puteoli, where we found brethren, and were invited to stay with them seven days. And so we went toward Rome." It appears that the centurion Julius was very accommodating towards Paul at this point. He allows the journey to transport his prisoners to Rome to be delayed for seven days because the Christians there had invited Paul to stay. Julius had been very impressed with Paul. Perhaps he became a Christian, but if he had, Luke most likely would have reported it. At any rate, this would have been an unusual thing for a centurion to do under the circumstances.

From Puteoli, they traveled on the famous Appian Way to a place called Appii Forum. It was a little over 100 miles from Puteoli and about 43 miles from Rome. By this time, word had reached the brethren in Rome that Paul was near, so they went to meet him. They reached him at Appii Forum.

Their presence was a great comfort to Paul because it indicated that he would be received favorably by the Christians in Rome.

When they reached Rome, the centurion had completed his task, so he turned over his prisoners to the captain of the guard. No doubt it was because of a favorable report from Festus and the testimony of Julius, that the authorities in Rome treated Paul with kindness. They allowed him to stay in a house with only one soldier to guard him.

After three days, Paul called together the leaders of the Jews to explain his situation; and they were anxious to hear what he had to say about the way they called a sect. "So when they had appointed him a day, many came to him at his lodging, to whom he explained and solemnly testified of the kingdom of God, persuading them concerning Jesus from both the Law of Moses and the Prophets, from morning till evening" (Acts 28:23). As was always the case, some believed and some did not.

"So when they did not agree among themselves, they departed after Paul had said one word: 'The Holy Spirit spoke rightly through Isaiah the prophet to our fathers, saying,

'Go to these people and say:
"Hearing you will hear, and shall not understand;
And seeing you will see, and not perceive;
For the hearts of this people have grown dull.
Their ears are hard of hearing,
And their eyes they have closed,
Lest they should see with their eyes and hear with their ears,
Lest they should understand with their hearts and turn,
So that I should heal them.'"

Therefore, let it be known to you that the salvation of God has been sent to the Gentiles, and they will hear it!" (Acts 28:25-28)

At this point, Luke brought his narration to an end. He says that Paul remained in his rented abode for two whole years and received all who came to him and preached the kingdom of God and the gospel of Jesus Christ with no one forbidding him.

The only logical explanation for this abrupt ending to Acts is that there was no more to write at this point. His narration had caught up to the time then present, so he closes the book with a description of Paul's work while he was in chains in Rome. What he does not tell is the fact that Paul wrote letters to Ephesus, Philippi, Colosse, and Philemon during those two years.

Discussion Questions
Chapter 18

217

1. Why do you think it is so difficult for powerful men to surrender their lives to Jesus? Have you ever known a government official who was a devout Christian?

2. Do you think Paul made the right decision to appeal to Caesar? Would Festus have released him if he had not appealed to Caesar?

3. Do you think any of the prisoners tried to escape when they made it to shore?

4. Do you think the centurion became a Christian?

5. Why was Paul's ministry at Rome not met with violent opposition from the unbelieving Jews? Did they not consider him a threat because he was a prisoner?

www.ingramcontent.com/pod-product-compliance
Lightning Source LLC
Chambersburg PA
CBHW060405310726
48976CB00003B/949